THE SEARCH FOR TK

D1208051

THE SEARCH FOR TK

Bobbi JG Weiss

CANDLEWICK
ENTERTAINMENT

Chapter 1

DOUBLE HUG

Kit Bridges stood at the door of TK's empty stall.

He's gone, she thought.

Lady Covington had warned Kit that if she didn't ride TK and compete in school equestrian functions, TK would have to go. "An unruly horse in the stable is both a hindrance and dangerous, to say nothing of the fact that no one is riding him," she had said.

So Kit had struggled to overcome her fear of riding, and she had succeeded. She had developed a relationship with TK, and she'd discovered that he wasn't unruly. Well, he definitely *was*, but not because he was a bad horse. He just had a more sensitive temperament than most horses. He had needed someone who understood his quirks.

That's where Kit had come in.

She had made amazing progress with TK after enduring weeks of peer tutoring with the seemingly perfect Elaine Whiltshire. She'd learned to ride TK through a dressage test, and after intense practice, she'd managed to guide him through a jumper course as well. She had struggled to catch up to the skill level of her peer riders at The Covington Academy for the Equestrian Arts, and she had tried her best to compete as required in the past weekend's House Cup competition.

But she had failed. After all her hard work, TK had balked, badly, at the very first jump. She'd almost gotten herself severely injured in front of the entire House Cup audience when he reared up in a panic. Because of her, Rose Cottage had lost the House Cup to the boys of Juniper Cottage. Because of her, the entire school's standing in the BSEA (the British Schools Equestrian Association) was now much lower than Lady Covington wanted. And because of her, TK had been taken away last night, just as Lady Covington had threatened.

Kit stared at his empty stall, numb with grief. TK was so much more than just a horse to her. He was her friend. He was a rebel, like she was. He had his own special way of doing things, and she had formed a bond with him that was so unusually strong that even she didn't understand it. But she could feel it, even now that he was gone. They had taken him away despite the fact that she needed him and he needed her.

Kit had lost so much in the last year, starting with the death of her mother. She and her dad had moved all the way from Montana to England in an attempt to start their lives anew, and though all the changes had presented their own difficulties, the move had proven to be a good one.

But now TK was gone, and Kit felt that horrible emptiness, that deep agonizing heartache, all over again.

Footsteps approached. Arms reached out and wrapped her in a warm hug. "How are you feeling today?" her dad asked, gently pulling away so that he could see her face. Kit's father, Rudy Bridges, had been hired as the school's equestrian supervisor, but to Kit's dismay, he had been unable to stop Lady Covington from banishing TK. Lady Covington owned and ran the prestigious riding school. She was the headmistress. Her word was law, and even

Rudy, the strongest and most loving man Kit had ever known, couldn't change that.

Kit tried to smile. "I want to know what our plan is."

Rudy thought about it. "Well, it's Monday. That means omelet bar day. I'd recommend the bacon and peppers. Then after that you have Latin class—"

"I'm talking about TK. How are we going to get him back? What's the plan?"

Rudy pursed his lips and silently pulled Kit into another hug.

Kit nudged back. "Why are you giving me the double hug?"

In her experience, the double hug never meant good news. She searched his eyes, hoping to see that spark of cowboy rebellion that meant he was willing to fight for her and TK against all odds. Rudy was the best dad in the world, Kit's champion and protector. Whenever she needed him, he was there for her. But the spark she hoped to see in his eyes wasn't there. She saw just one thing, and she didn't like it: sympathy. "No . . ." she said, not wanting to believe the truth. "Dad!"

"TK is dangerous," Rudy said. "He's unpredictable. Those are just facts."

"Mom always called *you* dangerous!" Kit exploded. "And you're definitely unpredictable! But we didn't ship *you* off to who knows where!"

"I know this is tough, kid. TK was a really important step—"

"He's not a step! He's my horse!" Kit tried to keep her voice from breaking as she added, "He's my friend."

"Kit, there will be other horses."

"You're supposed to be the one person who is always on my side!"

"I am," Rudy insisted. "I know it doesn't feel like it right now, but we'll be okay."

"Oh, *you* seem just fine already," Kit said. "Thanks!" She stormed out of the stable, her hands balled into fists. She had only one option left, so she decided to go for it. She stalked through the courtyard, across the field, past the practice arena, into the main school building, up the stairs, and straight to Lady Covington's office.

Barging through the door, she targeted her rage at the female figure standing by the window with her back turned. "You had better sit down because I have a lot of things to say to you! Sitty-downy things that—" Kit stopped dead as Sally Warrington, one of

Covington's English teachers, turned around. "Oh. You're not Lady C."

"Definitely not," Sally agreed, folding her arms, "and I think that may be to your advantage in this situation. Why don't we sit and take a moment to collect our thoughts?" Sally, who was always one to maintain decorum, calmly indicated two chairs.

Kit plopped down into one of them, too startled to argue. Maybe it was a good thing that Lady Covington wasn't there. If she had been, Kit would probably be expelled already. But now Sally was going to get the full brunt of Kit's anger. Kit knew that wasn't fair. The really awful part was that, at that moment, she didn't care.

"Perhaps a slightly calmer approach?" Sally went on as she lowered herself into the other chair. "Take a deep breath—"

"I'm already breathing, see?" Kit snapped, panting in demonstration.

"Goodness," said Sally as Kit felt her cheeks flush from the flood of too much oxygen.

"Okay, now I'm a little light-headed," Kit had to admit. "But that's good! I want my head to be nice and light! That vampire is *not* going to know what hit her—"

"Good morning," came a proper-sounding English voice. "Am I late for a meeting in my own office?"

Sally stood up respectfully as the headmistress entered. "Uh, Kit and I were just discussing . . ." She trailed off, forcing a small, stiff smile.

Kit wondered what Sally could possibly say to save the situation. She was a sweet young woman who cared deeply for her students, and her standards of behavior were high. But even if she risked a fib, how could it mask Kit's choice of words? It was pretty clear by circumstances who *vampire* had been aimed at . . .

"We were just discussing a series of graphic novels we enjoy," Sally suddenly resumed. "About immortals. And . . . now . . . Kit was going to *go*."

At any other time, Kit would have burst out laughing. Instead, she looked up at Sally in irritation, then over to Lady Covington as the headmistress asked her, "Is that true, Katherine?"

Kit opened her mouth to speak. No words came to mind.

"Well, spit it out," said Lady Covington. "This awkward silence, although a surprising change for you, is interfering with my very busy morning."

That did it. The headmistress seemed to enjoy constantly reminding everyone of how importantly busy she was, as if nobody else in the world was doing anything important or busy. *Fine!* Kit thought. *If you're so doggone busy, then let's cut to the chase!* "Where is TK?" she demanded, jumping to her feet. "I followed your schedule! I held up my end of the bargain!"

Sally quickly interjected, "I think what Katherine means is—"

Kit didn't want to hear it. The time for polite manners had ended when the vampire headmistress had taken TK away from her. "I can't believe you got my dad on your side," Kit said. "*That* I did not see coming. You're good, Lady Covington, I'll give you that. But you can't take away my dad *and* my horse!"

"Isn't it lovely that the students can feel comfortable enough to express their inner thoughts?" Sally offered in an apparent attempt to soften the situation.

Kit ignored her. *I'm up to my neck now*, she thought, *so I might as well see it through.* "Where. Is. TK?" she repeated.

"What time is it?" Lady Covington responded, casually glancing at her watch. "Eight thirty. I expect he's already in France."

"*What?*" Kit cried.

"He's been sold."

"To who?"

"To *whom*," Lady Covington corrected her. "To a lovely German family with a holiday home in France. There's plenty of land, and he'll be properly broken."

Broken? You mean his spirit will be destroyed! He won't be TK anymore! Kit found herself switching from anger to pleading. "His performance in the ring was my fault," she said. "He was in a mood, and I wasn't listening!" Silently, she added, *That's what Elaine told me, and according to you, I'm supposed to learn from Elaine, so listen to me, please!*

Lady Covington did not listen. "He has been sold," she said. "My decision is final."

Chapter 2

NAV-TACULAR PLANS AND WHILTSHIRIAN MISUNDERSTANDINGS

On any given morning, the Covington stables were a busy place. Students had to feed and groom their horses, muck out the stalls, sweep floors, clean tack and other equipment as needed, and fetch heavy bales of hay and alfalfa. At the same time, they had to keep an eye out for signs of any pest infestations in the stable and ailments in their horses. Students and staff workers hustled back and forth, greeting one another as they passed, commenting on the latest gossip, and in general, enjoying their chores. It was hard work, but it was satisfying. No one there had a desire to be anywhere else. Horses and riding were the reasons Covington existed.

One stall, however, was silent on this busy morning. The stall contained only a bale of hay, and on that bale slumped a very despondent Kit Bridges. TK's bridle lay in her lap, and as she stared out at nothing, her fingers gently caressed the leather straps. She sighed and closed her eyes.

A sound at the door made her open them again. Will Palmerston stood there. "Hey," he said. He seemed to want to say more, but when Kit remained silent, waiting, he just nodded awkwardly and walked away.

Kit knew what he wanted to say. *I'm sorry*. That's all anybody was saying to her. Everybody knew she was devastated, but nobody knew what to do about it except say *I'm sorry*. She was going to freak if one more person said that.

When Nav Andrada appeared, she steeled herself to hear it again. But Nav surprised her. "Hi. Any word from Anya?"

How refreshing to hear something different! Too bad Kit was feeling as depressed about Anya as she was about TK. Anya Patel had recently left the school, and Kit believed it was her fault.

During her time at Covington, Anya had been

keeping an incredible secret: she was really the daughter of a maharaja of India. She was a bona fide *princess*! But she had come to Covington to live, learn, and grow as a regular teenager because she didn't want to depend on the privilege of her social status. She became Kit's roommate and best friend, until recently, when Anya's secret had been discovered. As she had feared, people had begun to treat her differently. Most terrible of all, though, was that Kit had actually gotten angry at her for "lying." Only now did Kit understand Anya's point of view. *And now she's gone, too,* Kit thought dismally, clutching TK's bridle as she tried to formulate an answer to Nav's question. "I haven't heard *from* her exactly," she finally said. "Josh says she's in London, and that she's all right, so . . . that's something."

"Good," said Nav. "Um, I had a thought for you."

Oh, don't say you're sorry, please!

"Horses have papers," Nav continued. "TK's sale would have had to go through the registry. If we find the bill of sale, we find TK."

Kit's jaw dropped. "That's a great idea!"

"It's worth a shot," Nav agreed. "I'll find you at lunch for an update, okay?"

Kit could hardly contain her excitement. "Better than okay!" she cried. "Nav-tacular!"

Lunchtime rolled around. In the dining hall, Elaine Whiltshire sat at one of several tables, half a chicken sandwich with a side of tomato slices on her plate. When her loyal henchwoman, Peaches, joined her, Elaine said, "Peaches, I have some rather tragic news."

Peaches wasn't really a henchwoman. She was a fellow student. But Elaine considered her her personal assistant. Peaches did anything Elaine told her to do, no matter how sneaky. Not even Elaine knew why Peaches was so willing. But Peaches seemed fine with the arrangement, so Elaine took full advantage.

Upon hearing Elaine's warning about tragic news, Peaches said, "Oh, no!" Her expression grew sad. "But Mr. Mittens was so young! What about his nine lives?"

Elaine stared at her.

"He should have worn a helmet," Peaches declared, taking a carrot from her plate and nibbling it.

By now Elaine was used to the utterly bizarre

things that Peaches often said, but this one took the cake. "What? No!" She had to compose herself all over again so that she could announce with appropriate gravity, "I am unable to continue tutoring you in grammar."

"Oh, good!" Peaches exclaimed. Seeing the shock on Elaine's face, she backtracked with "I mean, *oh, bad*! Obviously my grammar is still in need of your splendiferosityness."

"Mangle the language as much as you like, Peaches, but I must go where I'm needed." As she said this, Elaine glanced over at the doorway. Her next project, handsome Will Palmerston, was entering the hall.

Peaches followed her gaze. "Ohhhhhh," she said. "You are needed in County Cute." She gave Elaine a knowing grin.

Elaine refused to let Peaches know that she'd hit the nail on the head. "That has nothing to do with it," she lied. "Will is an excellent rider, and I must ensure his ability to compete moving forward. Now, run along."

"But—"

Elaine cut her off. In her world, henchwomen did

not disobey orders. "You know where you're supposed to go," she said sharply.

Peaches hung her head like a scolded puppy, picked up her plate, and scuttered over to the table where Kit, Josh Luders, and Nav were sitting. Elaine was pleased to see her pursuing her ongoing assignment, which was to hear and report back any interesting news about the school cowgirl.

Elaine focused back on Will, annoyed to see him wave shyly at Kit, who waved back, equally shyly. "Will!" Elaine called, gesturing emphatically at the empty chair next to her.

Will slid into the seat Peaches had vacated, but he glanced back over at Kit.

"Um, so . . ." Elaine started, in an attempt to focus his attention on her. "Now that the Covington Cup is over, I wanted to offer to help you. I obviously couldn't help you before because, well, my main focus was beating your house."

Will was looking at Kit again, though Kit was now talking to Nav.

Elaine leaned in closer. "But now it's over," she went on, "and we're all back on the same team. I wanted to offer my assistance with something I know you're . . . troubled with?" She decided to end the speech as a question. That way she appeared hesitant, as if she was aware of the sensitive nature of Will's academic problems. He would jump up and run if she came right out and said, "Let me help you with your studies before you get yourself kicked out." She considered herself a master of subtle persuasion. Too bad it wasn't stopping Will from glancing at Kit yet again. Elaine waited, annoyed, until her offer suddenly hit him.

His eyes went wide. "Really?" he asked. "I didn't think you'd be into helping me with . . . this." Yet another glance at Kit.

Elaine yanked his attention back. "It's fine! I mean, we're friends, aren't we?" She was getting excited now. Will wanted her to tutor him! She'd had her doubts, but it looked like her plan was going to work. She was going to spend many delicious hours alone with Will Palmerston! And during those hours she was going to show him that they were made for each other. After all, it was obvious to everyone, right? Except him. Well, now she'd have a chance to change that. "So," she said, her voice giddy, "I'll get my books!" She reached for her tote, eager to get started.

"Books?" Will asked.

Why did he sound so confused? Then she got it. He was giving her a compliment, implying that she didn't need books to tutor him because she was so smart. How sweet of him! So she teased back, "Yes, *books*. They were created long, long ago, and they're filled with words. You'll love them!"

Over at Kit's table, Nav was holding up a folder. "This is what the registry looks like," he explained to Kit. "You see the—"

Across from Kit, Josh held up his cell phone. "If TK got shipped out of the country, then there's probably a record of that—if we know the name of the new owner."

Nav gave him a frosty frown. "Yes. That was my point."

"How do we get our hands on that kind of information?" Kit asked.

Nav began to answer, but he wasn't as fast as motormouthed Josh, who said, "Lady C's got to have a copy of the bill of sale."

"I was just about to say that!" Nav protested.

"Pick up your pace, brah. Look, if you talk like me, dude? You get way more stuff done."

Kit ignored the boys' one-upmanship game and thought out loud, "We just break into her office."

"You are very brave, Kit," said Peaches. "Like a girl in a novel!"

While Kit wondered what that was supposed to mean—and why Peaches was sitting with them and not Elaine, anyway—Josh said, "Except why make this harder on ourselves? I mean, why don't we just do the old distract-and-snatch?"

"Forgive me," Nav said politely, "but I don't speak Criminal."

"Aw, c'mon, roomie."

Kit saw that a proper demonstration was in order. She let out a big fake sneeze with a big fake, "Achoo!"

"Bless you." Nav, ever the gentleman, offered her his handkerchief. And as he did so, Josh snatched Nav's pudding cup and began to snarf it down.

When Nav noticed his dessert disappearing down Josh's gullet, he rolled his eyes. "Oh. Right. I get it. Do they just teach you this at birth in the Wild West?"

Kit realized something. "But wait, guys. I can't be anywhere near Lady C today, not after my blowout this morning."

"Hey, we got this—don't worry," Josh assured her. "We just need to find a way in."

Peaches spoke up, her eyes fixed on Josh's pudding cup. "Can I have the dessert?"

Josh held the pudding protectively. "No way, Peaches. Find your own scam."

Peaches aimed her response at Kit, not Josh. "What if I told you I could get you an appointment with Lady Covington? *Bystro*."

Kit had no idea what *bystro* meant, but Peaches seemed quite serious. Kit had always thought of her as Elaine's loyal minion, but the offer sounded too good to pass up. So Kit snatched Josh's pudding cup and handed it to Peaches. "I'd say you just scammed a dessert!"

Peaches started eating, giving Josh a sneaky, "Heh, heh, heh!"

Kit was glad to see that Josh took it well. At least the scammer knew when he'd been outscammed.

An hour later, Elaine entered the student lounge, excited about her first tutoring lesson with Will. He was due to arrive any minute. "All right, everyone out," she told the four students who were there.

They all glowered at her.

"Come on, you know the drill!" Elaine jerked her thumb over her shoulder to further indicate her wishes. "I need the space, and that means I don't need *you* in it, thank you. I'm sure you can find somewhere else to study. Spit-spot!" She clapped her hands as if she were commanding toddlers.

The students grumbled, gathered up their books, and left. Elaine smiled as she watched them go. It was satisfying to know that they understood who ruled the roost. She didn't enjoy ordering people about; that wasn't her goal at all. It was simply a matter of practicality. Those students could study anywhere. She, on the other hand, needed the lounge in order to help a fellow student. Her needs were more important.

She chose to conduct her lesson on one of the plush red couches rather than at one of the tables. Couches were more comfortable and therefore more conducive to teaching a peer, she decided. Especially a very cute one. She straightened the cushions and plumped up the pillows before setting her books on the nearby coffee table. Then, after straightening her uniform jacket and arranging her skirt so that it would fan out just right, she sat.

The sound of footsteps approached. Hastily she

grabbed her lip gloss and put some on, pressing her lips together to distribute it evenly. Perfect!

Will appeared in the doorway. She waved him over. "Hi," she said, a little breathlessly. Goodness, he looked handsome. She never ceased to marvel at how he could energize a room simply by being in it.

"Hi." Will plopped down next to her, dumping his backpack at his side.

"Um, so," Elaine began, trying to ignore the fact that Will's hair was all rumpled. It was so adorable that way. . . . "We'll just dive right in."

"Yep, sounds good."

With that confirmed, Elaine reached for her textbook and opened it on her lap.

Will frowned at it. "Oh. You want me to write this down?"

Elaine *wanted* to say, "Of course! This is a grammar lesson! If you don't write it down, you'll forget it!" Will was distractingly cute, but when it came to language skills, he really needed all the help he could get. But what she ended up saying was, "Um . . . yes?" She didn't want to scare him off.

"Fine," Will said. "Fine."

As Will rummaged for his notebook, Elaine began. "Okay, we'll start simply. What is the hypothesis in this conditional statement? 'If Walt drops Katie's books, he will pick them up.'"

Will stared at her as if she'd spoken in ancient Mycenaean Greek.

"A conditional statement is written as: if A, then B, where A is the hypothesis and B is the conclusion," Elaine supplied helpfully.

"Okay . . . so you're saying . . ." Will thought for a moment. "I need to pick up her books."

It was Elaine's turn to be confused. What was he talking about? "Let's try another one." She flipped through her text. "'If Walt takes good advice, he will be a raging success.'"

Will nodded, thinking. "So . . . if Walt . . . listens to the right people . . ."

"Which will be me, naturally. Then the conclusion is . . . ?"

"Then . . . it'll all work out for him. Success."

Elaine held back a sigh of relief. Good. He got it. "Brilliant!" she exclaimed. "Confidence and decisiveness."

"Confidence and decisiveness—that's your advice?"

Elaine nodded. "Always. Let go of the past. Start fresh."

Chapter 3

OPERATION BREAK-IN

Of all the students at Covington to suddenly leap into a distract-and-snatch leadership role, Peaches would hardly be Josh's first pick. He had her pegged as a total ditz—book smart, at least, because she'd gotten accepted into Covington, but personality-wise? A sweet but naive fool (she took orders from Evil Elaine, after all).

He was now discovering that he was way off base.

Once she'd gotten ahold of his pudding cup earlier that day at lunch, Peaches had proceeded to instruct him, Kit, and Nav to meet her by the staircase near Lady Covington's office that evening at precisely seven o'clock. When Josh arrived at 7:03, she turned to him and said in her cute chirpy voice, "You are late,

Mr. Luders. Bad boy. Five points off, and you get detention."

Kit and Nav snickered as Josh said, "What?"

Peaches ignored him. "All righty, is everybody ready? Then follow me, please."

Josh, Kit, and Nav followed her to Lady Covington's office. As they walked, Peaches told them, "Every month, as arranged by my governess for my mother and as a favor to my father, I help teach Lady Covington Russian." She held up a fat paperback book.

Josh found her statement hard to believe. "Really?" Peaches was *teaching* the headmistress? Yeah, right.

Peaches explained, "Apparently she has a long-time dream of biking from Moscow to Vladivostok."

Josh was relieved when Kit asked in a very confused tone, "*What* are you talking about?"

"Teaching Lady Covington Russian." Peaches reached the door to the headmistress's office and continued matter-of-factly, "Why? What are *you* talking about? If you want, I can teach you, too. Or I could teach you Italian or French, Spanish, Hebrew, Mandarin, Japanese—oh yeah." She grinned. "And Farsi."

"You do *not* speak all of those languages," Josh said. Not possible. No way!

Peaches replied with a sneaky twinkle in her eyes, "My dad's a diplomat."

Josh heard Nav mutter, "Ah."

"But you guys cannot breathe a word about this!" Peaches warned them. "If Elaine finds out that I have secret audiences with Lady Covington? She'll demote me. I'd have to hang around with"—she paused— "well, *you* guys."

Josh's ego took a massive hit.

"No offense," Peaches added, as if that could take the sting off.

Before the insulted trio could think of an appropriate response, Lady Covington opened her door. Josh scrambled back around the corner with Kit and Nav. He heard the headmistress greet Peaches in Russian, and the last word sounded like a name: *Pashkova.* Then the headmistress added in English, "Close the door behind you, would you, Penelope?"

Ha! So that was Peaches's real name: Penelope Pashkova! Josh began to wonder if this girl was more clever than anybody knew. He immediately saw that, yes, she was clever—she had left the door open! This was it! The chance she had promised! Josh jumped into action and slipped inside.

Peaches shut the door.

Okay, first he had to get to Lady Covington's desk and hide. Peaches gave him a chance for that, too—she practically threw herself into the chair that Lady Covington was about to sit in, forcing the headmistress to take the chair that would make her sit with her back to her desk. Excellent! Josh crawled to safety.

Meanwhile he heard Peaches say, "Shall we begin?" She tittered nervously, sounding like a little bird: "Hehehehehh!"

"Yes," said Lady Covington. She paused as Peaches tittered again. "Are you all right, Penelope?"

Josh peeked over the desk to see what was wrong. Peaches must have been more nervous by the situation that she'd expected because she kept making that birdlike tittering noise, a manic smile plastered on her face. "Oh," she assured Lady Covington, "I'm fine, hehehehehh!"

Lady Covington accepted the explanation and opened her copy of the same book Peaches had. She began to read in halting Russian. She could have been reading anything from a political biography to a superhero comic book. The Russian words floated past Josh's ears, meaningless, as he quickly but quietly riffled through stacks of papers, searching for anything that looked like TK's bill of sale. All he saw were forms and files that suggested the job of headmistress must be mind-numbingly dull. Nothing on the desk was any fun at all, just boring expense reports and supply lists and donor letters and *whoa—!*

Just in time, he caught the vase of yellow tulips that he'd knocked over. He recovered from a heart attack and placed the vase back on the desk, then looked up at Peaches, who gawked back at him, ready to freak.

"Hehehehehheh, I can't do this. . . ."

Lady Covington thought Peaches was talking to her. "Oh, am I that off this evening, Penelope?"

"Oh, no," Peaches said. "I'm just so wrapped up in the story, heheheh. I mean, imagine! A ghost! Hehehehehheh!" Her tittering was starting to sound hysterical.

Hesitantly, Lady Covington inquired, "Shall we continue?"

Josh caught Peaches's eye and nodded at her. He

still had a ton of papers to go through. She couldn't stop now!

Peaches seemed to get the signal and gestured for Lady Covington to continue reading.

"Very well," the headmistress said. Then, "Are you *sure* you're quite all right? You seem a little excitable this evening."

"Oh, no, Lady Covington. Uhhh—it's your Russian! I'm just so impressed with your progress!"

"Oh. Well, thank you."

Peaches tittered again as Lady Covington resumed reading. As she spoke a word that sounded like *blecch* to Josh, he found what he was searching for—an envelope marked RECEIPT CONTAINED. He held it up so that Peaches could see it and gave her a thumbs-up. Then he moved his finger in a big circle, indicating that she should wrap up the lesson so he could leave. He had no intention of squatting behind the desk for an hour listening to halting Russian. He didn't think Peaches could control herself for that long anyway.

In fact, Peaches lost it right then, letting out a loud, "Hehehehehehehe!"

Lady Covington regarded her with serious concern. "Dear girl, are you *sure* you're all right? You don't need to see the nurse?"

"No!" Peaches squeaked. "I just need to, uh, wrap things up!"

Josh saw that her cheeks were flushed. Poor Peaches looked close to fainting. Josh gave her a reassuring smile.

"Hehehehehehehe!"

Okay, reassuring smiles weren't a good idea.

Thank goodness Lady Covington stood up. "Perhaps that's for the best then."

"Okayhehehehe!" Peaches stood as well, clutching her book to her chest.

Josh prepared to make a dash for the door as soon as Peaches gave him an opportunity. Instead, Lady Covington opened the door to find Nav standing there. "Mr. Andrada," she said in surprise.

Nav stepped boldly into the room. "Am I too late?" he asked. "Have I missed it?"

"Missed what?" the headmistress asked. "This has turned into a very strange evening. . . ."

"I was hoping to audit your lesson," Nav said, stepping forward a little more so that Lady Covington had to step back—leaving Josh a clear path behind her out the door.

With silent thanks to Nav, Josh sneaked out.

Nav kept Lady Covington's attention on him.

"Peaches just raves about your progress." He added in his most suave voice, "Now, if you're ever inclined to learn Spanish . . ."

"Oh, no, my Spanish is actually quite perfect," Lady Covington boasted. *"Buenas noches, Monsieur Navarro."*

From his hiding spot around the corner, Josh could still hear the conversation. He slapped his hand over his mouth to keep from laughing. Riiiight, Lady Covington knew Spanish—*Monsieur* was French! Josh couldn't wait to post it on Chirper.

Nav, on the other hand, praised the headmistress. "Nailed it!" he said. *"Adiós, señora Covington."*

"Hehehehheh!" Peaches tittered helplessly, trotting out after Nav.

Kit was waiting for them down the corridor by the tuckshop. Nav had insisted that she move away from Lady Covington's office in case anything went wrong. Considering the disaster she'd already caused that morning, she had readily agreed.

Now Josh appeared with Nav and Peaches. He held out an envelope. "Got it!"

"We'll find TK if it's the last thing we do," Nav added.

Kit took the envelope, her heart pounding. Her new Covington friends were the best! She opened the envelope and unfolded the paper. "Oh, no," she said, skimming the contents.

"What?" asked Nav.

"This doesn't tell me where TK went. It's a bill for new curtains!"

Josh grabbed the paper and scanned it.

"Those curtains are very expensive," Peaches noted. "She should reconsider."

Josh slapped the paper down on the tuckshop counter. "I'm sorry," he told Kit. "It was the only receipt-like thing in her whole office."

"We'll figure something out, Kit," said Nav. "I promise."

"We have to." Kit tried not to be too disappointed. She knew they had taken a big risk for her already, but without their continued help, she wouldn't stand a chance of finding TK. "See you guys tomorrow," she said. "And thanks." She turned and left the group.

As she walked out of the school's main building and down the path leading to Rose Cottage, she heard the *tippy-tap tippy-tap* of Peaches's steps behind her. She appreciated the fact that Peaches was keeping her distance. Kit didn't want to be rude, but she wasn't in the best mood now that she was right back where she'd started from in her quest to find TK. *I'm surprised Peaches offered to help at all*, she thought. *She must really like pudding.*

It didn't surprise her that the *tippy-tapping* followed her into Rose Cottage. And since Peaches's room was across from her own, Kit wasn't surprised to hear the *tippy-tapping* follow her up the stairs. "Good night," she said over her shoulder, and moped into her room.

It felt so dismal without Anya. Kit tried to ignore the empty second bed, the empty shelves, and the empty desk and dresser on Anya's side of the room. With a heavy sigh, she set her bag down.

Tippy-tap tippy-tap! The door clicked closed.

Kit turned around to see Peaches grinning at her. "Okay, what's up with you? Why are you following me?"

"Elaine gave me to you," Peaches announced, as if it was something that happened every day.

"What?"

"Because you lost your horse. And Anya's gone.

She figured you could use, well"—Peaches struck a pose—"me!"

"You have got to be kidding me. *Elaine* is pitying me? Oh, this is the worst!" Kit flopped onto her bed, smashing her face into her big soft pillow. It was one thing when people did you favors because you were depressed. It was quite another thing for them to loan their own friends to you like library books.

Peaches *tippy-tapped* closer. "I can't really go back," she explained. "She threatened to confiscate my fuzzy slippers."

Right, Kit thought. *Peaches is as much a victim as I am. Thank you, Elaine, for this heartfelt complication.* Without raising her head, Kit pointed. "That bed is yours," she muffled through her pillow. "Sleep well."

Peaches *tippy-tapped* her way over to Anya's bed. "Good night, new best friend!"

That made Kit raise her head.

Perched happily on the bed and smiling like a goof, Peaches merely stared at her.

Kit felt like she was living with a cartoon. "Promise me you'll close your eyes? Eventually?" But for all she knew, Peaches sat like a grinning loon all night.

Chapter 4

WHEN GOOD ADVICE GOES BAD

The next morning, Kit walked to the dining hall alone. Peaches must have gotten up early, and frankly, Kit found that to be a relief. She wasn't interested in borrowing emergency friends, especially from Elaine.

She ran into Will in the corridor. "Hey," he greeted her. "Josh told me about his and Nav's little Russian spy act."

"Hilarious, right?" Kit laughed. Getting serious, she added, "I mean, I wish they'd gotten somewhere, but . . ."

"It's not going to help."

Kit paused. Why would he say that? "It might have," she said.

"I mean the whole idea." Will seemed to gather himself, as if preparing a speech. "If I were you," he said in a firm voice, "I would move on. Forget about the past and start fresh." He nodded as though mentally checking over what he'd said and finding it acceptable. Then he gazed firmly into Kit's eyes, his jaw muscles tight and his whole body tense.

"What?" was all Kit could say. Was he for real?

Apparently he was, though some doubt seemed to creep into his voice as he repeated, "I think you should move on . . . ?"

"Why are you acting like that?"

"I'm being decisive."

"You're being decisively *annoying.*"

"Yeah, but, I thought—" Will waved his hand around as if trying to catch what he wanted to say out of thin air. "I thought that's what you needed 'cause— you're a girl and all that."

"Because I'm a *girl*?" Kit expected flames to shoot out of her eyes. "I don't even want to know what that means!"

At this point, Will seemed so confused that all he did was shrug at her, his mouth opening and closing like a gawping goldfish.

Kit calmed down. "All I need is a friend. And if I don't get TK back, I honestly don't even know if I want to be here."

"Yeah, you're right," Will agreed.

"That I should leave?" With a growl, Kit stalked away. On a good day, Will tended to fumble with words, and Kit usually found it rather endearing, but this—*this* was way beyond fumbling! *He thinks I'm indecisive? He thinks I need somebody to tell me what to do? Because I'm a GIRL?* She felt like a teakettle full of roiling boiling water about to let loose with a window-cracking whistle.

What was Will thinking?

As the morning wore on, Will felt worse and worse about his conversation with Kit. He was so distracted by it that he almost flubbed up a math quiz, and history class turned into a real trial—Kit was in the same class, and she refused to acknowledge him the whole time.

What had he been thinking, saying what he'd said to her? Everything had come out wrong! He'd never meant to tell her that she needed someone to make decisions for her because she was a girl. He would never say a thing like that to a girl, especially one as strong and willful as Kit. And when he'd said, "Yeah, you're right," he'd been referring to her comment about needing a friend, as in, "Yeah, you're right, you need a friend, and I want to be that friend for you." He hadn't meant she should leave Covington. That was the last thing he wanted!

He couldn't have bungled things up more if he'd tried.

He needed to find Elaine. History class was about to end, and lunch was next. When class let out (Kit swept past him and out the door without a word), he hurried outside. Elaine was probably on her way to lunch, too, so he loitered around the door until he spotted her coming up the path from Rose Cottage, her big tote bag slung over her shoulder.

He trotted up to her. "Your advice was terrible," he said in greeting. "I'm pretty sure she's never going to speak to me again."

"What are you going on about?" Elaine asked. Then, "Oh, you got it! 'Your advice was terrible, *therefore* she's never going to speak to me again.' Very nicely done."

No, no, no, she wasn't following him at all. "I'm serious," he told her. "I really messed up."

"Look, don't be embarrassed. We'll get your grades up. There's no way you're leaving Covington."

A big neon DUH sign flashed in Will's head. "Ohhhh, you were *tutoring* me!"

Elaine gave him a flirty smile. "I know. We get on so well, it doesn't feel like work to me, either!"

Will glanced behind him at the practice ring where Kit had appeared to be headed after class. "All right, fine, I just need to—"

Elaine didn't give him a chance to finish. She seemed so pleased at how her *tutoring* was going that she slipped her arm through his, saying, "Dining hall?"—though it clearly wasn't really a question, as she steered him in that direction.

Will jerked his thumb back. "Yeah, but I should really—"

"Work hard to get your marks up?"

Oh, it was no use. When Elaine got like this, there was no way to stop her, so Will gave up. "Okay, sure. Let's go."

A special introduction was taking place in the practice ring. "Kit," said Rudy, "this is Coco Pie. Coco Pie, this is Kit."

Kit folded her arms and said nothing. She simply stared at the white mare before her, all tacked up and ready to ride.

Coco Pie swung her head around and blinked lazily at Kit through incredibly long white lashes. She was smaller than TK. She held her head at the same level as Kit's, and Kit could see right over her back. Her mane was cut short so that sections of it stuck straight up, and her forelock grew thick, giving her a cute blow-dry look.

"Coco Pie's a good horse, kid," said Rudy. "She's strong, gentle, responsive. And you've made so much progress just getting back into riding—"

Kit knew that her father was trying to help, but he didn't understand. "It's not just about riding," she cut in. "TK and I were a team. You of all people should know that. I'm not just going to jump onto some random horse!"

Coco Pie made a rumbling noise deep in her chest.

"No offense," Kit said to the mare. "You seem

nice, and . . . I like your whiskers." She figured that Coco Pie deserved a compliment. After all, it hadn't been her idea to get all tacked up only to be rejected by a complete stranger.

Rudy gave Kit one of his *I'm trying to work with you here* looks. Kit knew it well. It was the expression he wore whenever he was trying to get her to do something she didn't want to do. "Let's say you did find TK," he said. "Horses cost money. Do you have thirty-five years' worth of allowance to buy him?"

Why is he bringing up money? Kit thought. *That's not fair! I don't have any, and he knows it!* "I'd figure something out," she snapped. She knew she was bordering on disrespect. Her dad was only trying to help her stay in school. Oh, why did everything have to be so hard? "I don't care," she said, referring to money and Coco Pie and the impossible reality of her situation. All that mattered was TK. "I'm finding him!"

Even during lunch, Elaine tutored Will. In her view, his entire future now depended on her. Besides, it forced him to stay with her!

She carried his plate over to a table, saying, "So you could say that the peanut butter"—she indicated the contents of the plate—"is the conjunction in this sandwich. Why is that?"

"Um, because it's sticky?" Will ventured, following behind her like a cute little puppy.

At least, that's how Elaine thought of him—an adorable puppy's personality hidden beneath the surface of one very handsome face. "Yes!" she said happily. "Yes, think of conjunctions as sticky, just like your favorite sandwich filling!" They sat down at a table, and Elaine handed Will his plate. She wasn't going to eat. She just wanted to watch him.

Nav entered the dining hall and angrily headed for the buffet table, saying to Josh behind him, "The whole thing was my idea. If you hadn't jumped in like a china shop full of bulls, I might have gotten somewhere!"

"I'm just trying to help, roomie," Josh said.

"One, stop calling me that!" Nav had had enough. Josh was driving him crazy! "And two, stop trying to help!"

In his typical overly dramatic fashion, Josh

pantomimed getting an arrow to the heart. He jerked back, clutching at his chest. "Ouch, dude! Look, I thought me and you were simpatico, seeing as how we're roomies and all. . . ."

There was that word again! Nav clenched his teeth.

Elaine could hear Nav and Josh arguing, but she didn't care. What other students did in the dining hall was inconsequential—unless it created a situation that directly benefited her. So, ignoring the rising voices by the buffet table, she leaned in close to Will and purred, "I have a surprise for you."

"All right, yeah?" Will said, chewing.

Elaine nearly swooned. All he'd said was "All right, yeah," but the *way* he said it made her heart flutter. She had noticed long ago that Will Palmerston never seemed to get nervous or overexcited. He always appeared in control, and she found that very attractive. For example, right now he was staring at her with a stony, blank face. It made him appear terribly manly, and she couldn't wait to share her big surprise. "Pop quiz!" she announced, holding up a grammar quiz sheet she'd made. It was laminated, of course.

"You ready?" she asked him.

"Yeah, great." Will picked up his empty glass. "Do you mind if I get a drink first?"

"Sure." Elaine couldn't expect the poor fellow to eat peanut butter *and* take a pop quiz without something to drink, now could she? Besides, this would prolong the moment. She liked doing that, prolonging good moments. Feeling this good could last forever, as far as she was concerned.

Will reached the buffet table as Josh stomped away from Nav. Will figured they'd had an argument. As he began filling his glass with fruit juice, Nav sidled over to him and hissed, "Why did you trade rooms with him?"

Will replied, "We made a bet." Unfortunately, Will had lost that bet. That was how he'd ended up moving out of his nice big dorm room with Nav and moving into a smaller room with world champion snorer Leo Ducasse.

It had happened like this: During the House Cup

competition a week ago, Will had been itching to teach Nav a lesson after Nav had badly insulted him. So he'd specially tutored Josh on his jumping technique, helping him beat Nav in the jumping competition. Josh had done a good job, and Will had enjoyed watching Nav lose quite spectacularly. The downside was that Josh's price had been a room trade—Josh didn't like rooming with Leo, either. Thus, Nav had suddenly found himself with motormouth Josh in his dorm room instead of Will.

"Why wasn't I consulted in this bet?" Nav asked. "I had a stake in it, surely!"

Will debated how to answer. He couldn't tell the truth. If he did, Nav would find out that the whole mess was just a play for revenge. Nav wouldn't like that. So Will made his response vague. "Well, don't forget, mate—according to you, I'm messy, and I listen to my music too loud—"

"That's nothing compared to that guy!" In a low voice edged with disgust, Nav said, "He does *not. Stop. Speaking!* Particularly when *I* want to speak."

Will nodded. That sounded like Josh, all right.

"He calls me *roomie* or *dude*," Nav continued with a snarl. "I'm not sure if he knows my real name!"

"Oh, now, I'm sure he knows your real name,"

Will said with a grin. Seeing Nav so flustered was more revenge, and he was enjoying it. Still, a part of him—a small part, mind you—couldn't help but sympathize. Josh really did talk a lot. He could probably outtalk an auctioneer.

"And he won't stop bragging about the fact that he beat me at the Covington House Cup!" Nav went on. "He has videos!"

"Yeah, that does sound pretty vexing," Will admitted. Then he heard something that sounded like plates and cutlery getting pushed around.

"It *does* matter!" came Josh's voice. "It *does* matter! It *does* matter!"

"It doesn't concern you!" Elaine's voice countered.

Will and Josh turned to see Josh fighting with Elaine over—Will couldn't believe it—the pop quiz Elaine had made for him! Josh was stretching his arms over Elaine's head to get at it, while Elaine kept a death grip on it, struggling to pull it away. If the thing hadn't been laminated, it would have been ripped to shreds.

"And what are you doing with Elaine?" Nav asked Will as they watched.

That was a really good question, one for which

Will didn't have a good answer. "I'm not really sure," he said.

Elaine turned in her chair and hunkered protectively over the quiz paper. "You're going to break it!" she told Josh.

"Dude, you can't break paper! Just let me look at it! C'mon, chill!"

"But it's not for you!"

Will didn't need this nonsense. He pointed at Nav, then himself, then the door. Nav nodded, and they both sprinted out as the battle for the laminated quiz continued.

Chapter 5

PUSHED TOO FAR

Will and Nav parted ways once they'd escaped the dining hall, but now Will was faced with finding a place to go. He knew that the second Elaine noticed he was gone, she would hunt him down, and he didn't want to deal with her anymore, not without a break first.

He ended up charging through the tack-room door and almost knocking his riding instructor off his feet.

"Whoa!" Rudy cried in surprise, almost dropping the stack of clean saddle pads in his hands.

"You've got to let me hide in here," Will pleaded. "I just need five minutes without Elaine!"

That sparked Rudy's interest. "What's going on?"

Will opened his mouth to explain, then debated what to say. Rudy was Kit's dad, after all. "Okay, so I wanted advice about"—he fidgeted—"a girl . . . that I like . . . but Elaine thinks she tutoring me, and worse, now I think she might fancy me again."

Rudy gave him a weird look that looked as if . . . well, Will wasn't sure *what* it looked like.

He blundered on. "Yeah, it gets better, by which I mean it gets worse. So I actually used her advice on . . . the girl I like."

"And how did that go?" Rudy asked, setting the saddle pads on a storage shelf.

"How do you think? I'm hiding in the barn with you."

"Does this girl know how you feel?"

"No. That's the point. I acted like an idiot, and now she's never going to talk to me again!"

The last thing Will expected was Rudy's response: he chuckled.

"Thanks a lot!" Will snapped.

"I'm only laughing because it's happened to me," Rudy confessed. He picked up another pile of saddle pads. "I was about your age. Gabrielle was her name. I'd start tripping over myself and forget how to speak every time she was within a mile of me." He put the stack on top of the others with a soft *whump* sound. "And do you know why?"

Will had no idea what this Gabrielle had to do with anything. He shook his head.

"Because I liked her." Rudy chuckled again. "That's just how it works. I don't know why."

Well, what good was that? Will had a crush on Kit and acted like a complete fool whenever he was around her, and there was no way to fix it? That was simply how crushes worked? What kind of lame advice was that? "So what am I supposed to do?"

"I'd start by being honest with Elaine. You don't want her to get the wrong idea."

"That's the easy part. What about—?"

"The other girl? I think I'd start with an apology. After all, you are friends, right?" Rudy put an unmistakable emphasis on the word *friends*.

What did he mean by that? "Friends, yeah," Will agreed.

"Yeah," Rudy said. "Friends. For a long time." He put a hand on Will's shoulder. "A long, long time."

Oh. Will realized that Rudy knew exactly who the mysterious object of his affections was. He nodded, trying to look like he was casually accepting advice when, in fact, he was accepting Official Advice from the Father.

He had to find Kit right away, but he didn't know her schedule well enough to know if she had a class right now. The easiest place to check first would be the student lounge, so he headed there.

The second he poked his head through the door, Elaine said, "Hi!" She was seated at one of the red couches exactly as she'd sat during their first tutoring session. "I thought you'd forgotten about our study date."

Which, of course, he *had* forgotten. But now Will was glad that he'd stumbled into it. As much as he needed to straighten things out with Kit, he also needed to tell Elaine the truth. It wasn't going to be fun, but Rudy was right—it wasn't fair to let her keep hoping.

"I was thinking we could try something new today," Elaine said as he sat next to her.

"Yeah, um . . . " Will cast a glance around the room. Good, Kit wasn't there. Funny how he'd come looking for her and now was glad he hadn't found her. He cleared his throat nervously, wondering how to derail Elaine's plans without breaking her heart. "Do you mind if I start?" he asked as an idea came to him.

This seemed to delight her. "Well, aren't you full of surprises! I just knew once you got into the Whiltshire Study Method, you'd be hooked."

Seeing her so pleased made it all the harder for Will to forge ahead. "So," he began gently, "we'll go back to Walt."

"Okay."

"And we'll say that Walt has . . . a friend."

Elaine nodded, entranced.

"And we'll call her Frances."

"Okay."

This was so hard. Now that he knew what was really going on, he could see Elaine's crush so clearly. Her eyes sparkled with it. Her whole body radiated it. She was so filled with absolute crushiness that Will forced his vision to go out of focus on purpose, so he wouldn't see the details of her expression when he delivered the blow. "And Frances is really great," he resumed. "And she helps Walt with all sorts of things, because she really cares about him . . . as a friend." He tensed, feeling Elaine's full attention on him like a lead weight on his conscience. "So, to put this properly, Walt . . . likes . . . another girl." There it was. The blow was delivered.

It struck home. Elaine looked away.

Will blinked and brought his vision back into focus, feeling like a coward. Here he was, hurting a girl he did care about, just not . . . that way . . . and he was trying to avoid the consequences. The least he could do was be honest, both with her and with himself. "Um . . . and Walt just wants to make sure that he's clear about that . . . with Frances."

Elaine's eyes met his.

Will forced himself to go on. "And I mean, Walt really likes Frances as well, as a friend, and I really appreciate all your help tutoring. I just want to make sure there's . . . no confusion."

Elaine seemed flat and colorless now. Her features had gone slack, her happy smile gone. Moving with little jerks, no doubt caused by reining in her emotions, she began to collect her things—her textbook, pen, notebook, tote bag—while saying, "You'll have to excuse me. There's only so many times one girl can hear *we're just friends.*" She managed to look at him. "I'm very, very, exceptionally clear on that. If you keep bringing it up like this, I'll have to wonder if *you* believe it." With all her belongings gathered, she made a hasty exit.

Will watched her go, wondering if he was a good person or a really rotten one. At this particular moment, he wasn't sure.

Kit spent the early afternoon moping. When she'd left her last class, she'd decided to sit in the corridor near the main stairway to calm down and gather her thoughts. She was still there, though her thoughts remained distinctly ungathered. In fact, they were swirling willy-nilly around in her head so fast, she was feeling dizzy—thoughts about TK, where he might be, if he was being treated all right, if her dad would change his mind and help her find him, where *Anya* was, if *she* was ever coming back . . .

"I was disappointed that you didn't take Coco Pie for a ride."

Kit had been staring into space. She looked up at the sound of Lady Covington's voice. The sight of the headmistress made her instantly angry. "Well," she practically snarled, "I guess we're both disappointed, then."

Lady Covington tried again. "It's important for a rider's growth to diversify, to become comfortable on other horses."

Kit stood up. "I don't want to grow as a rider! I want TK!"

"I make the rules of this institution, not you. Covington is a *riding* academy. You *will* ride, or you *cannot* stay. Am I making myself clear?"

"Perfectly." Kit turned her back on the headmistress and walked away.

"Katherine, come back here! Katherine, I'm talking to you!"

Talk all you want, Kit thought as she left. *I'm not listening.*

Rudy stood before Lady Covington's desk listening to a lecture, and as usual, it made him feel like *he* was the student in trouble rather than his daughter.

"She had no right to speak to me like that," the headmistress finished hotly.

"I'll talk to her," Rudy promised, "but first I need you to reconsider this whole TK situation—that's all." He knew TK was trouble. That was clear. But it was also clear that Kit's connection with the ornery gelding was the only thing holding her together right now. Lady Covington refused to even consider that selling him may have hurt Kit more than she intended and in ways she hadn't anticipated.

As a father, Rudy could see that his daughter needed to be taught a lesson, but Kit was a wild spirit, like her mother. In horse training terms, you don't tame a spirited animal with threats. You don't take away things in which it finds comfort. You have to lure the animal *to* you, earn its trust, and make it *want* to cooperate. With patience and love, you have to show it that obedience brings reward, not punishment. Otherwise the horse will flee, if not physically then at least mentally. You will never be able to connect with it, and the animal will be useless for any kind of meaningful work.

Lady Covington, however, believed in strict control, period, and she expected it from her staff as much as from her students. In terms of her decision to sell TK, she would not budge. "It's too late for that," she said. "Who runs things, Mr. Bridges? You or your teenage daughter?"

"You don't get it." Rudy sighed. He truly didn't

want to argue with his boss, but why couldn't she at least try to see things from another point of view? "We're a team," he said, putting as much emphasis as he could into those words because they defined his relationship with his daughter, a relationship that worked, especially now that Kit's mother was gone. He and Kit were both still trying to recover from total devastation. Their little family of three had been like a three-legged stool, whole and well-balanced. But now that one of the legs was gone, the stool kept falling over. If TK could be a temporary third leg on the stool, maybe that wasn't so bad. "We're still figuring things out," he explained, "and I—"

Will burst through the door. "I'm really sorry to disturb you, Lady Covington, and sir," he added to Rudy, "but it's Kit. I needed to talk to her, and I went to her room and the student lounge and the classrooms and—I looked everywhere! And—she's gone."

Chapter 6

ROOMIES, FRIENDS, AND BESTIES

Kit stood before the closed door of Room 148 in the Hampshire Hotel on Leicester Square, in London. It had been quite an interesting trip from Covington all the way to this room. She should have been excited and happy—she was about to see Anya again! But she was nervous.

Would Anya want to see her?

She knocked on the door. When it opened, there stood Anya, casually dressed and looking as sweet as ever. The second Kit opened her mouth to speak, the words just tumbled out: "Hi. My name's Kit. I'm wondering if we could be friends?"

"What are you doing—?" Anya began, only to switch to "Why are you—?" and then ending with "You're in London!"

"Lady Covington sent TK away."

Anya immediately sprang forward and wrapped Kit in a hug.

Kit hugged her back, soaking in the presence of her best friend. She had missed Anya so much! "I'm really sorry we had a fight," she told Anya in mid-hug. "I didn't mean it, and then you were gone, and I needed to talk to you and only you!"

Anya took Kit's hand and led her into the room. "First, tell me what happened."

Now that Kit was getting support from her friend, her emotions threatened to unravel. She'd been successfully holding them in check all during her journey. Now she could barely choke out, "She said TK was too dangerous, and Dad actually agreed with her!"

Listening, Anya sat down on the soft hotel bed, pulling Kit down with her.

Kit allowed herself to be led, still pouring out her story. "He's clearly lost his mind! And then Will said . . . well, Will said weird stuff about moving on and that I should leave."

Anya's eyes grew wide. "He said that?"

"I think so. He wasn't exactly clear."

"Oh, Will . . . " Anya furrowed her brow.

"This whole thing is the worst thing that's happened to me since I came here," Kit said. "Well, besides the fact that *we* got in a ginormous fight, and you left the school."

A look that might have been guilt flashed across Anya's face, but she didn't say anything about it. She pressed for more about Kit's predicament. "What are you going to do?"

"Lady C said she sold him. All I know is that he's somewhere in France." Kit tried to seem firm and confident as she finished, "So I'm going."

"And I'm going with you!" said Anya.

Kit grinned. "I was hoping you'd say that! When do we leave?"

"I think your families would feel differently about that plan," came a familiar voice.

Kit turned to see Madhu standing at the door. Kit had met Madhu weeks earlier and had believed her to be Mrs. Patel, but it had turned out that she was actually Anya's governess. She was currently giving both girls a stern frown, but Kit knew that Madhu had a lighter side. She could be pretty funny, and Kit had already seen how dearly she loved Anya. Kit pinned her hopes on those facts as she commented, "But who says we have to ask them?"

Out of the corner of her eye, Kit saw Anya give her governess a hopeful smile.

Madhu lifted her chin a bit so that she could look at the girls down her nose. Kit had seen adults do that before, as if it was a way to show their authority. It worked, too. Madhu seemed to be deeply pondering the situation. Kit knew that whatever she decided would become law.

Back at Covington, Rudy paced in the student lounge, talking on his cell phone. "And she's safe?" he asked his caller.

Sitting at a nearby table, Nav, Josh, Will, and Elaine were studying, but Rudy figured they were also listening to his call. They had probably guessed, as he had, that Kit had run away from Covington to look for her horse. Rudy had been beside himself, so when he received the call from Madhu from London, he had nearly collapsed with relief. "Does she know how worried I've been?" he asked Anya's governess, his voice rising. "We've been looking everywhere!

I thought—" He paused, forcing his voice back down. "Anything could have happened. . . ."

"She's fine, Mr. Bridges," Madhu told him. "I can assure you, she will be well taken care of."

"I have no doubt about that, ma'am," said Rudy, "but you tell her to be ready for some pretty large consequences, yeah?"

"I believe she's aware."

Rudy sighed. "Thank you for calling me. And for taking care of Kit."

"It is my pleasure. Shall I put her on the phone?"

"No, I'm not ready." That was the honest truth. "I need to think about what I want to say to her. Let her have the night before she faces my parental wrath. Thank you. Bye." He hung up.

"She's okay," he told the four students at the table. "Till she gets back into my sight. After that, I'm not making any promises."

"We're all very happy to hear it, sir," said Nav.

Rudy nodded and left, muttering, "All the way to London . . . She's a brave one, that girl."

Elaine watched Rudy leave. Then she tapped at her laptop keyboard, commenting, "She was only gone a couple of hours. Why is everyone so upset?"

Josh replied, "Knowing Kit, a lot of crazy action could have happened in a couple of hours."

That didn't matter to Elaine. "It's not exactly like her donkey's roaming the streets of London," she pointed out.

"No one can find him?" Will asked.

"I'm looking into a new lead," said Nav. "I spoke with my father. He has a contact. A scout for horses. They always know where a horse of good breeding ends up."

"These are the kinds of things you can do when you're him," Josh quipped to Will, and they both laughed. Then Josh said, "Actually, Elaine, I'm glad that you're here. Could you do us a favor?" Like a magician, Josh reached into his backpack and presto! The coveted Covington House Cup was in his grasp. He waved it at Elaine. "Gather round the cup, boys! *Our* cup!"

With delighted hoots, Will and Nav leaped from their chairs and joined him as Josh tossed his mobile to a very stern-faced Elaine.

Josh saw her expression and rubbed it in. "That's the *Covington House Cup*, ladies, just sayin'."

Will rapped his knuckles against it. "Such a solid win, yeah?"

Elaine picked up the mobile, got to her feet, and sauntered closer as if positioning herself to take the photo they wanted.

Sure that she was going to do their bidding, Josh, Will, and Nav posed for the shot: Will stuck out his tongue, Josh gave a cheery hang-loose sign, and Nav grinned a little maniacally and pointed at the cup, just to drive home the point that Elaine and Rose Cottage were *loooooooosers*.

It was all so typical of the male specimen, in Elaine's view. Boys simply couldn't help but act like children. It was in their DNA, she supposed. They never quite matured, unlike females. "You know," she told them, "no one likes a sore winner. Which means that people must really hate you." With that, she dumped the mobile into the House Cup. It landed inside with a metallic clang.

She walked out, though she glanced at the three stooges one last time out of morbid curiosity. Josh had retrieved his mobile, and they were taking a three-man selfie. "Everybody say pumped!" Josh cried.

Will broke his pose. "Pumped? Seriously?"

"I don't say *pumped*," Nav declared in a superior tone.

Josh sighed. "Fine. Whatever. Just smile and bask in victory!"

That got the guys back into the mood, and they mugged shamelessly into the camera as Josh clicked a picture.

Elaine shook her head and left.

Back in London, Kit and Anya were facing Madhu. Their fate had yet to be determined. "He didn't want to talk to me, huh?" Kit asked, referring to her father.

Madhu responded, "He just needs the night to clear his head. You gave him quite a fright, young miss."

Kit didn't want to ask the next question, but she couldn't stop herself. "Am I grounded?"

"Because then I suppose we would have to go to bed early," Anya said. "Sigh."

Madhu regarded the two girls. Kit put on her

best smile, hoping that might help. She didn't know Madhu very well, but since Anya thought she was pretty cool, maybe their punishment wouldn't be too bad. Maybe.

"Given that you have been separated," Madhu finally said, "I was thinking we could allow you one night of . . ."

Kit swallowed nervously.

"*Supervised* fun," Madhu finished.

Anya burst out in giggles, and Kit hopped up and down in glee. *We can celebrate being together again!* Kit thought happily. Not everything in her life was going well right now, but this was more than she could have hoped for!

They plopped down on the big hotel bed and spread out a menu before them. Anya picked up the phone and called room service. "Room 148," she said. "Can we order two burgers, vanilla ice cream"—Kit gestured and Anya nodded—"and cookies. And crisps!"

"Pizza!" said Kit.

"And pizza!"

Fifteen minutes later, they received their order on a rolling cart. They wheeled it to the bed and lifted big silver lids off several plates. The burgers looked scrumptious and came with lots of condiments: ketchup, brown sauce, three different kinds of mustard, mayonnaise, relish, pickles, onions, and even horseradish! The pizza had everything on it imaginable—*except* anchovies. They got a huge bowl of crisps (which Kit knew as potato chips), a plate of tarts and biscuits (which of course Kit called cookies), and a plate piled high with chips (French fries to Kit). Kit was starving after her long, anguished journey. She and Anya dug in, talking with their mouths full and giggling and generally acting like goofballs.

Anya turned on the TV and ordered one of her favorite horse movies, the classic 1944 version of *National Velvet*, starring Elizabeth Taylor. "Her eyes were really that color," she told Kit when the first close-up of Taylor appeared on the screen. "Natural violet eyes, can you believe it? Not contacts!"

When a scene came showing Velvet riding her horse, the Pie, at a full gallop across an open field, Kit told Anya, "I want to ride like that!" through a mouthful of pizza.

"You will," Anya told her. "You will!"

They watched the whole movie, stuffing their faces and commenting on the action the whole time. Kit knew it was a miracle they didn't choke with all the laughing and pillow throwing going on. Madhu had to come in a couple of times and tell them to quiet down, but she always left with a little smile on her face.

"Do you think she secretly wants to join us?" Kit wondered.

"Oh, I'm sure she would love to," Anya said, "but it's far too undignified. I'm surprised she's letting us get away with it. Then again"—she pointed at Kit—"she doesn't have her very own Kit to show her how fun is done!"

When the movie ended, Kit sighed. "That was so good that I *almost* forgot about TK for a minute."

Anya took out her mobile and typed for a moment. Then she gave the mobile to Kit, saying, "There. I put it on Blurter."

Curious, Kit read the message. "'Lost. One slightly insane horse. Answers to TK. Mostly black. Entirely moody.' That's not very specific, is it?"

"I *said* he's probably in France and likes to eat paper."

Madhu appeared yet again. "Lights out, girls. It's very late."

"Yes, Madhu," Anya obediently replied.

The governess turned out the room light and left.

With the room now dim and everything quiet, Kit knew this was the time for the Big Talk. There were important matters to clear up between them. But which one of them would speak first?

Anya did. "I'm sorry I lied to you."

"I know," Kit immediately responded. "I'm sorry, too. It just felt like everyone was in on the secret except me."

"And I wanted to text you as soon as I left, but I couldn't figure out what to say. I'm so sorry."

"Wait," said Kit. "Is that a *royal* apology?"

"No princess jokes," Anya said seriously.

Kit couldn't hold in her laughter anymore. She cracked up.

Anya punched her in the arm. "That was mean!"

"No, that was funny!"

"Then I'll banish you from my kingdom, or at least from my swish hotel room."

"No way! Not until I've pillaged this place for all the room service you super-fancy people have got."

Anya didn't mind the teasing now. "Let them eat chip-n-dip!" she said.

Kit snorted. Anya took the same history class she did, and they had been studying the French Revolution. Most people thought Marie Antoinette had said, "Let them eat cake," when she'd heard that the French peasants were so poor they had no proper bread. But Kit and Anya had learned that, although the average French person at the time was indeed poor—that's why they'd started the revolution!— Marie Antoinette had probably never said those words.

Kit tried to imagine *Princess Anya* wearing a huge white powdered wig like Marie Antoinette. The mental image made her laugh again.

"What?" Anya asked her.

Kit was about to explain when Madhu, sounding fed up, called from the other room, "Go! To! Sleep!"

Both girls pressed their lips closed, holding back more giggles. When they finally settled down, they got into bed and pulled the covers up, facing each other. "I felt like I could tell you anything," Kit confessed. "And I just wanted you to feel the same way."

"I do," said Anya. "And . . . you're my best friend."

"Do you think you would ever go back? To Covington?"

"I would like to."

"Great. Because I'm thinking that heading to France isn't such a good idea."

"I'll come back with you. Tomorrow!"

"Good! And then we can start finding another way to get TK back." A terrible thought came to her. "And also, I have to face Lady C. She probably has the dungeon all prepared for me."

"Are you fellas ready for movie night?" Josh asked Nav and Will that night. They'd finished dinner and were on their way to Juniper Cottage. "Leo Ducasse is screening an epic mixed martial arts marathon in the student lounge." He flew into a kung fu pose — or what he thought looked like a kung fu pose. "Wooo-*haw*!" he cried, slashing with a fist. "It's gonna be pretty sick."

Nav shook his head. "I'm going to study," he said.

Josh pretended not to hear the insult buried in Nav's words. Nav had once told them that he kept his grades up because he studied every night instead of wasting time on other things. Josh thought that was fine and dandy, but in his view, martial arts flicks were just as important as school studies. How else was a guy going to learn to protect himself from an attack? You couldn't learn those cool moves from a math book. Josh already had the yells down pat. He could "Haaii-*yah*!" with the best of them, as he had demonstrated moments earlier.

Nav, however, seemed to have no interest in learning the art of self-defense. Neither did Will, since he told them, "I'm going to my room, seeing as how Leo won't be there. He's an awful roommate. Snores worse than my nan."

"Speaking of which," Nav said, thrusting his hands into his pockets, "I was wondering if we could discuss reversing this little room dance you've done? I would like Will back as my roommate now, please?"

Josh mimed getting an arrow to the chest for a second time, trying to impress upon Nav how much his words hurt. He grabbed at his chest with a dramatic gasp. "Brah, you wound me!"

Will shrugged. "Yeah, well, it might be time, right? Fun's over, Josh."

Josh wasn't about to let these two ruin what was,

for him, a brilliant situation. "No, no, no, no, no," he said. "The bet was not I-get-your-room-for-a-few-days. The bet was I-get-your-room-for-the-rest-of-the-year!"

"All right," Will agreed, "but Nav's saying he doesn't want you there."

"And since when do you care about his feelings? You"—Josh jabbed his finger at Will—"*you* specifically trained me because you wanted him beaten. No, no, no," he recalled, "you said *humiliated*." Only then did Josh realize what he'd done. Will was staring at him, looking horrified.

Josh wondered if sometimes he talked too much. Well, it was too late now. The secret was out.

It was Nav's turn to get an arrow to the heart. "Is that true?" he asked Will.

Will's horrified look turned to a guilty one. He refused to meet Nav's eyes.

"Very sportsmanlike, William. And very kind." Nav looked genuinely hurt.

"I just thought you needed to learn a lesson," Will said uncomfortably.

"I learned *something*," Nav stiffly informed him. He turned to Josh. "Come on . . . *roomie*. We've got a movie to catch." He walked away.

Josh wasn't sure what to think. Now Nav was calling him roomie, like a real roommate! But he'd frowned when he said it. That couldn't be good. The frown was aimed at Will, though, so maybe things were okay after all. Conflicts between bros didn't bother Josh as much as they did others. For him, bickering was how you dealt with most people. So he threw a grin at Will, hoping Will would grin back. He didn't. So Josh dialed it down to a half grin, shrugged, and followed Nav.

As far as Josh saw it, Will had started the whole thing in the first place. Let *him* figure out how to recover from a backfire.

Chapter 7

COMING BACK TO COVINGTON

Early the next morning, a shiny black town car arrived at the entrance to The Covington Academy for the Equestrian Arts. It slowly traveled up the long gravel lane and turned a wide circle in front of the entryway, where it stopped.

The back door opened, and Kit and Anya got out. Both of them clutched the straps of their tote bags anxiously, worried about how they would be greeted. Kit was sure that her dad would yell at her in front of everybody and that Lady Covington would then rip her to pieces with a speech containing very sharp words.

The two girls entered the main building. The first thing Kit noticed was the absence of Lady Covington.

Oh, thank you, universe, thank you, thank you, thank you, she thought. Then she saw Rudy, standing as tense as she'd ever seen him. *Here goes nothing.* "Dad?" she said, and then she winced, expecting a flood of scolding to follow.

Rudy stepped forward and drew his daughter into a tight hug. He didn't say anything. He simply hugged her as if he would never let her go.

Kit snuggled her face into his shoulder. "I'm sorry!" she said, and she meant it. This wasn't one of those times when she could just blurt out those words and get away with it. She could feel the raw stress and worry radiating from her dad, and that was a punishment in itself.

The look on Rudy's face told Kit that he accepted her emotional apology. He knew her well enough to know when she was faking it, and he knew she was not faking it now. "I'm not going to yell," he said softly. "I'm not going to scream. I'm not going to lock you in your room. Just — don't do that again." He had his hands on her shoulders, and he shook her a little bit. "Ever," he finished.

Under the circumstances, it might have been wise for Kit to remain silent. But she felt so bad about what she'd done that the words came tumbling out. "I just really wanted to find TK, and I needed Anya!"

Sally Warrington, their English teacher, stepped forward, her arms full of books. Kit hadn't noticed she was there. "All right, spit-spot, you two. We've got a great class to jump straight into."

"What about Lady Covington?" Kit asked warily.

"She will call you when she's ready for you."

"Oh, great," Kit snarked before she could catch herself. "I love suspense."

Anya continued to clutch the strap of her tote, now with both hands. "Really?" she said in a small voice. "I don't like it all that much myself, not if I'm in trouble."

Sally made a soft sound of amusement and headed for her classroom.

Rudy motioned for Kit to follow. "Go on. I'll see you later." As Kit and Anya obeyed, he added, "Be good, both of you."

The second Kit and Anya entered the classroom, Josh leaped up from his desk. "The girls are back!" he cried. "Hey!" And he lunged at them, pulling them into a three-way hug. Kit was so surprised by this that she burst out laughing. Anya did, too.

"And the fun score of this school just went up two thousand percent!" Josh proclaimed as he stepped back.

Nav came forward. "Oh, did you go somewhere?" Then he grinned and also gave them a hug. "We missed you."

"Jeez, guys," said Kit. "We went to London, not Timbuktu!"

"I did miss you all, though," Anya told the class. She had been gone much longer than Kit, and she spoke so sincerely that everybody smiled at her.

Except Elaine. Kit noticed how Elaine had kept her head down, ignoring their warm reception.

"Ladies, take your seats, please," instructed Sally. Everyone sat in their assigned places. "Our next writing project will explore *narrative voice*—writing from within another perspective. In order to find those voices, first we will begin by researching our family tree. Choose an ancestor who interests you."

Kit was tickled when Nav spoke right up. "A difficult choice. There's Uncle Paolo, who rescued the president from quicksand. And there's my great-grandmother who flew solo around the world."

Kit chimed in, "My mom was from England,

actually. She always said she'd bring us back. But we never made it. . . ."

"Sounds like we have some excellent choices," Sally said. "I would like to note that the backgrounds of our students are varied. Some of you may have rather humble roots; others may come from titles or dynasties."

Kit noticed how Sally glanced at Anya, who gave a little gasp, but Sally quickly resumed her instructions.

"What we are most interested in is the *person*. Let's have fun with this, and don't worry what anyone else will think." She nodded to indicate that the students should start thinking of who they wanted to write about.

Kit peeked over at Will. She could have sworn he'd glanced at her, but now he stared down at his notebook as if thinking hard on their assignment. She didn't have to think at all. Kit was going to research her mom, naturally.

A student entered the room to give Sally a note. Sally took it and opened it up, reading. "Katherine, your presence is requested in the headmistress's office, please."

And this is how the suspense ends, Kit thought. She

rose, grabbing her purse and tote. "See you later," she told everybody. "You know, if I'm alive and stuff." She handed her things to Anya, who took them without a word, probably already knowing that Kit didn't want the burden of heavy bags while confronting the headmistress. Kit might have to make a speedy escape out the window or something.

Now that she was unburdened—physically, at least—Kit hurried out. The last thing she wanted to do was make the situation worse by showing up late.

Elaine watched Kit leave, wondering how was it that everything ended up revolving around her. Kit wasn't a top student, her family wasn't important, and she was, quite frankly, complete rubbish at riding. She was an embarrassment to the school, in Elaine's humble opinion. Yet every time Elaine turned around, it was *Kit Bridges this* and *Kit Bridges that*. It made one wonder how such a boorish American managed to capture such attention. If her peers had any sense at all, they would rally around competent students, students who had talents that could pull the whole class up with them. Students like Elaine, for instance.

But, no, it was always the cowgirl. At least her stupid donkey was gone.

Elaine felt her phone vibrate. She knew it was against the rules to use mobiles during class, but it was merely lying on her lap. She sneaked a peek at it to see who had sent her a message. All she saw was a photo: Josh sitting at the dining hall's head table, right in front of the Covington banner, "feeding" chocolate cake to the big silver Covington House Cup!

In anger, she slammed her phone down.

"Elaine," said Sally, "we don't read our phones in class."

As Sally took Elaine's mobile, Elaine snapped, "Can you confiscate his, too, then?" She indicated a way-too-innocent-looking Josh behind her.

Sally ignored Josh. "Come on," she said to Elaine, forcing Elaine to follow her up to her desk, where they could discuss the matter in private. She looked at the photo on the mobile's little screen. "Oh," Sally said. "I would hope they could have a tad more grace after winning."

"It's not even the winning," said Elaine. She liked Sally, and so said with full honesty, "I just miss the celebration you always put together for us after we've won." How embarrassing to admit such a child-ish thing, but winning was such a lovely feeling, and Sally's victory parties really were special, and she missed it all so much!

A dejected expression crossed Sally's face. "Well, after all your hard work and hard training, you girls do deserve a treat."

Elaine was still stuck daydreaming about past victory parties. "One scoop pistachio ice cream, one scoop raspberry ripple, girls-only film festival in the common room . . ." She sighed. "I just wish they'd stop rubbing it in."

Now Sally spoke in a strange impish tone. "You know what they say—pride goeth before a fall."

Elaine snorted. "If that were true, then Josh and the other Juniper boys would have fallen off the edge of the earth by now."

"Perhaps," Sally said, still in that odd tone, "but they may yet be surprised by a fall from their pedestal."

Meanwhile, in Lady Covington's office, Kit was sitting and enduring a long lecture. "These rules exist not only to protect the reputation of the school, but also to protect *you*. Your actions were reckless, selfish, and inconsiderate. You worried your father half to death!"

"What's between me and my dad is between me and—"

Slap!

Kit jumped, but it was only the sound of a book landing. Lady Covington had dropped it on the desk in front of her. "This is the Covington Rule Book. I would like you to learn it to the letter."

Kit had a copy of the rule book but hadn't exactly studied it in detail. It looked like it was forty pages, tops. As punishments went, this was pretty mild since Kit was good at memorizing. "Okay, sure—"

Again she was cut off. "In particular, I would like you to pay attention to Rule 421, which states, *All students, unless injured or otherwise prohibited physically from participation, will ride.*"

"But you sold my horse!" Kit blurted out. Wasn't that the reason for this whole miserable situation?

"I sold *my* horse," Lady Covington corrected her. "If you do not follow these rules, Katherine, I will have to expel you. Would you like to leave Covington, Katherine?"

Oh, boy, here was an opening if ever there was

one. There were so many different ways to answer this question that, for a moment, Kit lost control of her voice and couldn't say anything.

Did she want to stay at Covington? *The better question is, where can I go if I don't?* she thought. *Dad still has a job here.* She had no idea what England's regular schools were like, but she doubted they were as nice as this place with its enormous dorm rooms and fabulous food. Yes, she had to wear a uniform, but she was used to it now. That alone amazed her.

But could she force herself to accept another horse besides TK? Coco Pie was . . . well, doggone it, she was dull! But maybe, just maybe, her dad was right about the white mare. Maybe Kit needed to ride a calm, dependable horse for a while before, lest she fall off and got her foot stuck in a stirrup for a second time. She didn't want to repeat *that* nightmare ever again. Maybe practice on Coco Pie was the answer after all.

The headmistress stood behind her desk, waiting for an answer.

Kit double-checked her thinking and felt satisfied. Did she want to leave? "No, Lady Covington."

"Then you will ride. Tomorrow."

"Yes, Lady Covington."

"If you do not ride tomorrow, you will leave—" Lady Covington's eyes widened, and she cocked her head. "I beg your pardon?"

The old Kit would have laughed at the adult's obvious shock. The old Kit would have found this whole discussion pointless and insulting. The new Kit did not laugh, and she realized that this discussion needed to come to a positive close.

"I'll do it," she said.

Now it was Lady Covington's turn to lose her voice.

The next morning, English class consisted of research time. Everyone worked on their family tree projects while Sally meandered up and down the rows, checking on each student's progress. Books, notebooks, and laptops were open, and the sounds of typing and scribbling filled the air.

When Sally reached the opposite side of the room from Kit and Anya, the two girls quickly bent over Anya's mobile. "I got a bunch of replies back to my Blurter post," Anya whispered. "This guy says he saw a black horse in Miami."

"If TK is lounging poolside, I'm going to be so mad," Kit teased.

With a snicker, Anya whispered the next comment on her post: "This girl says her nickname is TK. Not very helpful."

"In her case, it stands for Totally Killing me with the random."

"We'll just keep putting it out again and again, you know?" suggested Anya. "We're bound to get some information eventually."

Kit shrugged. "Yeah, from somebody in the Bahamas who says he saw a black horse mermaid flopping on a deserted beach."

Anya giggled.

"Girls," Sally scolded, eyeing them.

Anya put away her mobile, and both girls went back to work.

Two rows from them, at the very front desk, Elaine opened her textbook and stopped dead. A photograph lay between the pages, a photograph of a certain Josh Luders in *her* room reclining in *her* bed—with the Covington House Cup! And he was *kissing* it!

She wanted to cry out, *"Eeewwww!"* A change of bedsheets was definitely in order now, along with a liberal application of spray disinfectant. Maybe she'd burn some incense after that to make sure no trace of *eau de Luders* remained. Behind her, she heard Nav's distinct chuckle and Josh's trademark snort.

"Oh, there's our photo!" Josh stage-whispered to Nav, loud enough for Elaine to hear. "So weird that it ended up there!"

Over her shoulder, Elaine said, "I always find the best victories come with unexpected rewards. You're going to love yours."

Josh and Nav went silent.

Elaine couldn't wait for them to find out. In fact, she was smiling when, at that moment, Rudy Bridges entered the classroom. He removed his Stetson as Sally said to the class, "Attention, please. Mr. Bridges has an announcement for some of our boys."

"I have news for Juniper Cottage," said Rudy. "After learning that it is a tradition to reward the House Cup winners, I'm lining up a treat for you all tonight."

Josh, Will, and Nav hooted and clapped. "Pizza and video games!" Josh crowed, and he leaned toward Nav. "Hey, you want to split a pepperoni, roomie?"

Nav gazed up at the ceiling as if seeking divine aid. "Please don't call me that."

A totally delighted Elaine noticed that Sally also wore a smile—a rather vengeful one—as Rudy further explained. "I'm still ironing out the details with Lady Covington, but I wanted to give you all a heads-up so you can get your gear ready."

Oh, what a glorious moment! Elaine nearly squirmed with warm fuzzies as Nav, sounding wary, asked, "Excuse me, which *gear* are you referring to?"

"Camping," Rudy answered as though it were clear as crystal. "You're not going to get far in the wild without it."

"I am so jealous!" Kit piped up. "Camping with my dad is awesome!"

"I went camping once in France with my cousins," Will said. "It was really good. We had this awesome yurt thing."

"A yurt?" asked Kit. "Aren't they those big round tents with furniture in them?"

Defending his yurt, Will declared, "Yeah, but we only had *cold* running water."

"Not quite, I suspect, what Mr. Bridges has in mind," said Nav.

"It was still outside. We went fishing and stuff.

Anyway, when have you ever slept in anything other than a feathery bed?" Will directed the question to Nav, who glared back at him.

Rudy regarded the bickering boys. "Looks like we could use some team bonding here, anyway," he commented.

Elaine couldn't resist it anymore. This was simply the most wonderful conversation she had heard in quite a long time, say, ever since Rose Cottage lost the House Cup! She turned in her seat to face the so-called winners. "Ooooh, camping! Sounds fun, boys. I'll be thinking of you while I'm tucked up cozy in bed tonight."

When she turned back around, Sally was struggling to contain laughter. They exchanged a look of triumph. Yes, order had been restored at Covington.

Revenge was a sweet treat, indeed.

After English class, Kit went to the student lounge to research her mother's past. However, things quickly went pear-shaped, a British slang term that meant that nothing was working out at all.

When Will sauntered up, munching on his favorite

prawn-flavored snack crisps from the tuckshop, she said to him, "This is so weird. Westingate, the place where my Mom grew up? It doesn't seem to exist."

Will's mouth was full, but he answered anyway. "Maybe you got the wrong name?"

Kit shook her head. "Nope. I checked with my dad and everything. She used to talk about this nearby beach she went to as a kid—Wilco Sands. But I can't find it, either."

"Sometimes places change," said Will.

Kit thought it over. Maybe he was right. Maybe Westingate had been some tiny village that later became part of a larger town or something. Things like that happened in America, so they probably happened everywhere else. But how was she supposed to do a report on her mom if the information wasn't there?

Will interrupted her thoughts. "How did it go with Lady C?"

That was one question that Kit could easily answer. "I have to follow all the rules, or I get booted out of Covington."

"You'd think forcing a runaway to *stay* would be a better punishment," Will mused, stuffing more crisps into his mouth.

Was that supposed to be a joke? Kit decided it had to be. Will's idea of humor kind of went sideways compared to most people's. Kit was no runaway. Although she now knew that rushing off by herself to find a horse in France hadn't been the brightest move she'd ever made, Kit still considered herself a brave adventurer. *I do not run away from my problems*, she thought proudly. *I run at them. And sometimes into them. Which kind of hurts when they turn out to be walls, but hey.* Out loud, she added, "And I have to ride . . . another horse, I guess."

"But you can't. You already tried. You don't remember fainting at the sight of a little pony?"

Kit almost got angry, but this was Will, after all. She just grinned. "You sure know how to reassure a girl."

Will looked properly embarrassed. "Elaine says I'm awful at talking to girls. I think I'm awful at talking in general, really. Like, about feeling-y stuff. You know?"

"I get it. Have you met my dad?"

Will laughed, fiddling with the crisps bag. "I polished TK's tack for you. For when he comes home? 'Cause you're going to get him back, Kit. I know you will."

Kit beamed at him. Finally! This was the Will she lo—err, this was the Will she liked so much, the Will who believed in her. "I have no idea how," she confessed, "or where to start, but I'm not giving up on TK. Not now, not ever. So thank you." Her throat tightened up as she added, "For not giving up, either."

This time when she smiled at him, Will smiled back.

Chapter 8

BRO TIME
AND BIGFOOT

R iding class.

It was time for Kit to go to her dad's riding class.

She had managed to zombie-walk her way through lunch with Anya, but Kit had hardly heard her friend's happy chatter. All she could think about was the totally awful disaster-to-be that would occur after lunch: riding class.

Usually she and Anya went straight from the dining hall to their room and dressed for class together, replacing their academic uniforms with their required Covington riding gear: tan breeches instead of skirts and tights, a warm blue jacket with red side panels over their regular shirts and blazers (and those totally dorky school ties, which Kit called their Covington baby bibs), tall black riding boots instead of the usual black tasseled loafers, and of course, their helmets.

Today, Anya dressed alone. Kit just wasn't sure she could ride another horse, even though she'd promised Lady Covington that she would.

"Do you remember what you told me?" Anya asked her before leaving. "How horrible it was when I left Covington? Well, if you don't ride, then *you'll* have to leave, and I'll miss you." Tears appeared in her eyes. "I'll miss you so much! So you have to try, Kit. Promise me you'll try to ride."

The heartfelt plea almost made Kit cry, too. "I'll . . . I'll do what I can," she said. It was all she could promise.

Anya looked like she understood. "Okay. Maybe you could get dressed and show up, at least? That way, maybe Lady Covington will see that you intend to try, but you're just not ready yet." She gave Kit a hug and then hurried out.

Kit flopped onto her bed. *It doesn't matter what stupid clothes I wear*, she thought. *The clothes aren't the problem! Getting on any other horse than TK is the problem!* But she thought of what Anya would go through otherwise. *And you promised Lady C you would ride*, she reminded herself.

She got to her feet. "I'm going to do this!" she told the empty room. "I have to do this, not just for me but for Anya, and my dad, and"—she smiled— "and for you, Mom." She gazed up at the ceiling. "You never gave up on anything, did you? If you wanted to achieve something, you went for it. I don't remember ever seeing you back off or hearing you say *I can't*." Kit squared her shoulders. "And neither will I!"

Fifteen minutes later, Kit finished tacking up Coco Pie in the stable. The little mare turned out to be quite a prankster. She nose-bumped Kit several times, nickering playfully and lipping the frayed edge of Kit's cable-knit sweater.

"I never meant to insult you," Kit babbled as she put on her riding helmet and led Coco Pie outside. "It's just, you're not TK, you know?"

Coco Pie's ears flicked back, and she snorted.

"Sorry. I did it again—I insulted you." Kit stopped. "I'm going to need your help, CP. I mean, really truly. Will you do your best for me? Please? I'll never insult you again. In fact, I like your whiskers even more than I did before."

Coco Pie raised her head, looking Kit up and down, taking Kit's measure. Then she nudged Kit in the chest and nickered, as if to say, "No worries. I've got your back, little rider."

Kit glanced around to make sure nobody was watching. The coast was clear, so she wrapped her arms around Coco Pie's neck. "Thank you." Then she continued to the practice ring, giving herself a quiet pep talk as they walked.

When she reached the ring, Rudy was critiquing Josh's posture while the boy rode Whistler past him, first one way and then the other. "That's it, Josh," she heard her father say. "Good. Much better."

Kit heard the words, but they held little meaning. Her father was a blur, while Josh and Whistler were a bigger blur. The rest of the class, lined up along the far rails with their horses, were more blurs all mushed together. Kit's heart was hammering, and she felt her body go stiff and heavy with dread the closer she got to her dad. "TK will come back, and I'll ride him," she kept repeating to herself. "But today I'm going to ride CP. I'm going to ride. I can do it. I'm going to ride. . . ."

"Kit," said Rudy in surprise when he saw her.

Kit thought she might faint. "Hi, yeah, I'm going to ride, I, uh, I have to." Her words came out as feeble half whispers.

Rudy leaned closer. "You okay?"

"Uhhh, yeah, I'm going to be fine. I'm going to ride. I have to, so I'm going to ride. I have to." After repeating herself, she tried to take a deep breath, but the air wouldn't go in. She tried again, determined to stay strong, but it was so hard, just *so hard*. There. Good, she got one good breath in. That was a good start, breathing. Yeah, breathing was good.

"Okay," said Rudy, closely watching her. "Well, let's just go slowly, huh?"

Slowly? How could he possibly want her to go slowly? "There is no slowly," she said, her desperation giving her energy. "I've wasted enough time already, and he's getting farther and farther away every day, and *she* wants me to ride, so I'm going to ride!" Kit spun on her heel and glared up at the second floor of Covington's main building. It was where most classes took place, and it was where Lady Covington's office was located.

Rudy's eyes narrowed as he glanced at the window, too.

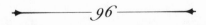

She's standing right there, Kit thought. *She's watching, so I can't mess this up!*

Her dad held Coco Pie steady as Kit took her position at the horse's side. Coco Pie was short enough that Kit didn't need any help mounting. *Grab the saddle, lift your left foot into the stirrup, swing your right leg over, and sit!* she thought as she accomplished each move.

She saw a look of hope in her dad's eyes, but once she was in the saddle, every sense Kit possessed cried out *Noooo!* Coco Pie, for all of her cute mannerisms, was the wrong horse. *All horses are the wrong horse!* Kit thought. She clutched the reins, trying to force her heart to slow down, trying to breathe. "It's not the same. I can't do it." Her arms tingled in warning, and her legs felt tight, and her chest turned to ice, and she had to get out of that saddle and back to ground level before she cracked into pieces so tiny that nobody would be able to put her back together again. "No, I can't. I just . . . I can't . . ." Once her feet were back on hard soil, she yanked off her helmet. "I just, um, need a breather!"

She ran away before anyone could tell she was crying.

Kit was still crying by the time she got to Rose Cottage. Ten minutes later, she was still crying as she lay sprawled on her bed, alone. Once again, she had failed. She had tried to ride, as Lady Covington had ordered her to, and she had failed.

TK was gone. Soon she would be gone, too, expelled from Covington. What would her dad do? What would he say? What *could* he say? He had watched her fail! It was that simple! She had failed! She was Kit Bridges, Big Fat Failure Girl!

Someone knocked on the door.

The last thing she wanted was company. She debated yelling out, "Go away!" but maybe it was important . . . like somebody delivering a note from the headmistress's office saying, "FAIL FAIL FAIL FAIL FAIL FAIL! But thanks for trying. Buh-bye!"

When she opened the door, Lady Covington stood there, wearing a jacket and scarf. "Come along," the woman said briskly. "We're going for a ride."

"I can't," said Kit. What else was there to say? "I'll never ride again. Not without TK."

The headmistress spoke softly. "Pack your tears away. We're going."

Didn't the woman ever listen? "I don't have TK!

And any other horse feels like a betrayal, so I can't meet your rules or conditions or whatever you call it."

"I know your thoughts and feelings, Katherine. It's time to go." She held out a helmet.

Kit was caught off guard — it wasn't a riding helmet. Well, it *was*, but not for riding horses. "This is a bike helmet," she said, reaching for it.

"Sharp as ever," the headmistress quipped. "Come on."

Later that afternoon, Rudy stood in the stable courtyard, waiting for the Juniper boys to arrive with their gear. It was time to start their house victory hike to a beautiful little spot by a stream that Rudy had been told was perfect for overnight camping.

Several boys had already arrived, appropriately geared up. Rudy didn't have to worry about them. But the main troublemakers of Juniper Cottage? They had yet to arrive.

He finally spotted Josh and Will approaching. Josh had clearly been camping before. He wore sturdy hiking boots and carried a backpack that appeared to be pretty stuffed with — well, Rudy could only hope it contained useful, practical items and not, say, twenty bags of marshmallows. Will, on the other hand, must have expected another yurt to be available at their camp.

"Sneakers and a comic book," Rudy noted. "Do you plan to survive the night, son?"

"This is all we had when we went camping in France," Will responded.

Rudy decided that the joys of nature would teach Will more than a lecture ever could, so he said nothing—until Nav appeared. "Nicely done!" he exclaimed. Nav was decked out in a rugged raincoat and hiking boots, and he was carrying a small pack and a bedroll. "I didn't think you'd know the first thing about camping."

Suave as ever, Nav whipped off his very expensive-looking pince-nez sunglasses. "Thank you, Mr. Bridges," he said. "Now, who's going to carry the rest of my belongings? Or should I call my driver?" As he spoke, some Juniper Cottage boys whom he'd recruited set down a collection of large cardboard boxes.

"What's all this?" asked Rudy.

"A portable television, a Blu-ray player, a

battery-powered fridge, a solar-powered shower . . ." Nav gave Rudy a self-satisfied look.

Josh pointed straight up. "My money's on cold showers, boys. Those clouds aren't letting Mr. Sun through anytime soon."

Everybody looked up, including Rudy. The lovely blue sky of a few hours ago had definitely clouded up, and those clouds were growing darker.

Will adopted a casual pose. "That's all right. I can handle a little bit of rain."

"So can I," Nav said, his tone challenging. "I've survived monsoons."

"I'd like to see you survive a wet weekend in Wales," Will retorted.

"I'd like to see you trek across the Argentine pampas in forty-degree heat."

"I'd like to see you two stop bickering!" snapped Rudy, though Nav's comment actually sounded pretty impressive. This was England, so Nav was talking forty degrees Celsius, which translated into 104 degrees Fahrenheit. That was pretty hot!

Will looked unimpressed. "It's not my fault if he can't handle coming in third."

"You betrayed me!" Nav declared. "Though

I ought to thank you, because I'd rather be stuck living with Josh than dealing with your two-faced behavior!"

Josh, ever stuck in the middle, said, "Dude, what? *Stuck* with me? I thought roomies were supposed to have each other's backs!"

"Well," Nav said, glaring at Will, "so did I."

Rudy observed this word war between his charges and knew he could never stop it. These guys had to work it out between themselves. His interference would only make it worse. So, as thunder began rumbling in the distance, he briskly organized his hikers and herded them to the trailhead.

The winds picked up, and the clouds grew nearly black. Rain fell in torrents, cold and sharp, and it kept on falling as Kit parked her bike next to Lady Covington's in an alcove near the school's main building. Headmistress and student then ran giggling to the front door, took off their coats, and hustled upstairs to Lady Covington's office, shivering. Kit feared her fingertips would freeze solid and fall off, but the office fireplace flickered with lively and wonderfully hot flames. *She must have arranged to have it ready for when we came back all wet,* Kit thought. *She planned this whole thing out—for me?*

"I thought you were way too ladylike to go skidding through the puddles and mud like that!" Kit said, putting her helmet down on the table.

"Being afraid of a little dirt shows signs of poor character. One must be willing to muck in no matter what the weather."

They stood before the fire, rubbing their hands. "When I was little," Kit said, "my mother used to send me out into the rain on purpose. She said no matter how wet you get, you can always get dry. Maybe she meant the same thing."

"Perhaps." Lady Covington pushed strands of wet hair from her face and loosened her drenched scarf. "You know, when I was younger, I rode my bicycle through the entirety of this country, from the most southern point in England all the way up to the northern tip of Scotland. And every night, I would set up camp." She laughed, picking up a blanket from the sofa. "One night we had a huge thunderstorm. It was really quite frightening and also very soggy. But, oh, the sunrise the next morning! I'd never seen anything like it!" She wrapped the blanket around Kit's shoulders. "And yes, I did get dry eventually."

Kit digested this information, holding the blanket close. Just that morning she had wanted to scream her lungs out at the woman standing before her, and now Kit just gaped at her in awe. Lady Covington had taken her out on a *bicycle ride*! Through the *countryside*! They'd ridden along smooth paths, bumped over uneven trails, and dodged their way down tree-edged roads where overgrown branches whipped their faces and leaves threatened to tangle in their wheel spokes.

When the storm had started, they'd kept right on going, sometimes pedaling right into the rainfall so that the cold fat drops stung their cheeks and forced them to squint so hard Kit could barely see in front of her. One time, as they'd raced down a steep hill, Lady Covington had actually yelled out, "Whoohooooo!" At least, that's what Kit thought she'd heard. Through all the wind and rain she couldn't be certain, but what she'd heard had either been the headmistress or a coyote — and England didn't have coyotes.

Lady Covington's voice broke through Kit's reveries. "It's impolite to stare, Katherine."

Kit realized her jaw had been hanging open.

"Oh, I'm sorry, I just—*you*! Biking! Camping! I can't compute!"

With a chuckle, Lady Covington directed Kit to a small table where a tea service waited: a hot teapot, two cups and saucers, milk, sugar, and a plate of warm biscuits.

Kit sat down, still overwhelmed by everything that she'd discovered. "It's like finding out Bigfoot is a real thing!" she blurted out. Once the words were out of her mouth, she realized that she'd just called Lady Covington Bigfoot.

Oops.

The headmistress let it slide. She had something more important to say. "As much as I enjoyed my bicycling adventure, eventually I had to return to my responsibilities . . . which is what I intended to teach you this afternoon."

Kit blinked. Their bike ride had been some kind of lesson?

Lady Covington went on. "I really do want you to stay at Covington, Katherine. But it does require some participation on your part."

Kit huddled in her blanket, holding her cup of hot tea with both hands. "I was participating," she said. "I got on a horse. That was huge for me! Maybe you don't understand how huge. After the accident, my mom never pressured me to ride. She said that I would find it on my own, and I did. At Covington. With TK. And now"—she gazed into the steaming cup—"he's gone."

Lady Covington thought a moment. "You're right," she said.

Kit's head threatened to spin. Here she was, sitting with the headmistress of the school after they'd enjoyed a totally outrageous bicycle trip in a torrential rainstorm. They were sharing tea and talking like adults, being open and honest, while their clothes were still damp and strands of wet hair hung in their faces.

Up to this point, their interactions had focused on spotless uniforms and perfect business suits, formality and discipline, orders and obedience. And now, suddenly, Kit was beginning to see her school administrator differently. Lady Covington was a *person*. She could be nice! And now she'd just said two words that Kit never in her wildest dreams expected to hear from her: *You're right.*

She was stunned.

Lady Covington continued, "Perhaps I didn't understand how huge it actually was."

"Well, it was," Kit managed to say. "And I really want to stay at Covington. I'm just not ready to ride, and I know the deal was that I had to do it today but—"

"But you did." Lady Covington indicated their riding helmets lying on the office couch. "You rode a bicycle."

Is she kidding? Kit thought. *Is she making a joke?* Kit did a double take at the helmets. *Is she breaking her own rule?!*

"I know how difficult this has been for you."

"And TK. Don't forget TK." Kit went out on a limb here, but if she was really going to be truthful . . . "I think he deserves another chance," she said.

"I hope one day that you'll understand that I sent him away for your own good." Lady Covington didn't use her usual tone of authority to say this. She spoke with honesty.

Kit appreciated that, but it was still hard to talk about her equine friend. "I just really miss him."

"Moving on is not forgetting."

Forget TK? Kit thought. *Never! I don't forget the ones*

I love. That made her think of her mother, and that made her think of her school project. "Hey, maybe you can help me," she said, setting down her tea. "I'm doing this research for my family tree project, and I was going to do it on my mom, but—"

"Oh," Lady Covington interrupted with a strange expression on her face.

Kit didn't notice. She was too wrapped up in her idea now. "But I can't seem to find where she was from. Westingate?"

Lady Covington said, "I've never actually heard of that."

"I've looked everywhere, and my dad is sure that's what she told us. Are you sure you've never heard of it?"

Lady Covington stood up. "Excuse me." And without explanation, she left.

Kit gaped at the door. "Lady Covington!"

No reply.

It was all too much, way too much. "What did I say?" Kit yelled at the empty office. It seemed the storm clouds had made their way inside.

Outside, rain continued to fall, wind continued to blow, and thunder continued its distant rumbling. And inside a tent, smack in the middle of it all, sat three grumpy teenage boys.

At first, Rudy had thought that the boys needed to work their problem out by themselves, but more and more he suspected they might never manage it. He'd have thought they were smart enough to see that he'd put them in the same tent on purpose, but were they speaking to one another? Nope. They were moping. Maybe he could give them a little nudge in the right direction. It wouldn't hurt to try.

He squatted down, unzipped their tent flap, and poked his head in.

There sat Will, Josh and Nav, all ignoring one another.

"So, we've settled on the silent treatment, huh?" Rudy asked.

Josh and Nav threw frowns at him while Will pointedly continued reading his comic, *The Hunter*, by flashlight.

Rudy began his plan with a tiny nudge. "Fine," he said. "Ruin the whole night for yourselves."

"Actually," said Josh, "I think *you* kind of ruined it, Mr. B."

Nav nodded. "It was your duty as the experienced camper to check the weather forecast prior to departure."

Will closed his comic. "Yeah, I know you don't think I know anything about camping, but I'm pretty sure it's meant to be *outside.*"

Well, at least he'd gotten them to agree on something, even if they were wrong. They *were* outside. Technically. Rudy had been forced to reject that beautiful camping spot by the stream—school rules regarding "inclement weather" and whatnot—so he'd set up camp under one of the school's big event tents. It wasn't as if the boys cared one way or another. They knew as much about real camping as he did about billionaire estate planning.

If only they could see that getting back to nature wasn't the only point of camping. The camping experience was also about sharing time with friends and enjoying the little things in life, the basics, those simple things that people usually ignored in the hustle and bustle of modern living—things like conversation, laughter, and the wonders of just being *alive.*

He nudged them toward that idea by saying,

"Well, yeah, part of camping is about being out-doors, but it's also about . . . what do you call it? Bro time?"

Will and Josh burst out laughing. "Bro time?" Will snorted.

Nav winced. "Please don't speak like Josh, Mr. Bridges. One is more than enough."

Good, they were talking about one another instead of him. Now to trick them into talking *to* one another. Otherwise they'd never get over their argument. Rudy knew about teenage boys, having been one once, so when the next idea popped into his head, he knew it was the right strategy.

He needed to unite them against a common enemy.

He pretended to get angry. "Well, excuse me for trying to enrich your lives! I've had it with all your buggin'!" He withdrew his head and zipped the tent back up. "Later, skaters!" he snarled, and walked away.

There, that should do it. He'd purposefully bungled his slang, and they were already laughing about it. Excellent. Next they'd start talking about how lame the camping idea was and how there was nothing to do, and maybe, just maybe, they would get creative and actually *think* of something to do.

Like pay attention to one another.

Rudy grinned. Yeah, they would be friends again in no time.

Chapter 9

DR. JOSH, REPORTER DAISY, AND MR. PALMERSTON

K it chased after the headmistress.

"I'm sorry!" she said, trotting alongside her because the woman was walking down the hallway with the briskness of a tornado. "What did I say? Lady Covington, I don't understand!" All Kit had done was ask if she had ever heard of the town Kit's mom was from.

The headmistress stopped abruptly. "I have no idea where Westingate is! I am not an encyclopedia, nor am I your homework buddy! If the information isn't available, perhaps it was never intended to be found!"

Whoa, what was going on here? Lady Covington was so riled up that Kit automatically got riled up, too.

"But my mom wouldn't have lied! So why would she say she's from a place that's not real?"

"How would I possibly know the answer to that?" The headmistress calmed down. "Just drop it, Katherine. Go to bed."

Kit had thought the corridor was empty, but a cheery voice called out in a cockney accent, "Hello, there! Hi!"

Lady Covington immediately transformed into the official headmistress. "May I help you?" she asked, her voice fuller and more confident than before.

A woman, maybe twenty-five years old, walked up to them. She was definitely a character, wearing a blouse with big cascading ruffles in front, six-inch pencil-heeled boots, and an adorable knitted cat-ear beanie. "Daisy Rooney," she said, holding out a hand. "From *Dish Quarterly*?"

"Oh!" Lady Covington responded. "We weren't expecting you until morning. How delightful!" She shook Daisy's hand.

"Soz to just pop in on you," said Daisy. "I wanted to poke around a bit, you know, have a peek?" She turned to Kit. "Could you manage a quick tour?"

"That won't be possible," said Lady Covington. "She was just on her way to the dorms. Curfew."

Kit liked this crazy Daisy person. She was definitely a fellow mischief maker. "We could walk together," she offered, shaking hands with the reporter. "I'm Kit."

"That won't be necessary, Miss Rooney. I would be delighted to give you a tour and to share with you some of our famous Covington hospitality. Come along." The headmistress began to lead the way down the corridor.

Kit liked the reporter even more when she dropped back to say, "We'll catch up tomorrow, yeah? I totally know about getting a dress-down by a teacher. I was an expert at it." She winked. "Still am!"

"Me too!" said Kit. "We'll compare notes."

With a nod of agreement, Daisy hastened after Lady Covington.

Josh felt trapped. Here he sat in a little green tent (underneath a huge white tent, of all things), smashed between a sulky Nav and a grumpy Will. "Dudes, this tent is too small for all your bad vibes."

Nav ignored him and spoke directly to Will. "I can't believe you set me up to lose. To Josh!"

"You were being such a jerk about the fact that I

couldn't ride, I had to make the impossible happen."

Josh threw his hands in the air. "Can you stop talking like you're both so surprised that I could win?"

"I'm not surprised," Nav told him. "I'm just . . . annoyed. I don't like to lose."

Will nodded. "Neither do I."

Josh wanted to say, "So who does?" but he knew that would only fan the flames. He preferred to try to smooth things over between his buds. "It's the worst, yeah. But," he said with pride, "when you think about it, none of us are losers compared to Rose Cottage. We totally kicked their butts!"

"We're clearly a superior team," Nav agreed.

"Except Kit and Anya," Josh thoughtfully continued. "They're all right. If they were here, we could be roasting s'mores!"

Silence.

Ohhhhhh. All this time, Josh thought the big problem was Nav's lousy cup ride because of Will, but there was something more going on here. Josh detected the spark of *girl trouble* in the air. "Look, dudes, the doctor is in, and Dr. Josh kind of feels like you guys are still fighting about Kit even when you're not fighting about Kit. You know?"

Nav responded with surprising sincerity. "I think

it's noble to have feelings for a girl. But perhaps it's even more noble to have a teammate." He looked at Will. "And a friend."

"Yeah, well." Will fidgeted. "The gentleman might be right. Maybe it's time we called a bit of a truce?" He held out his hand.

Nav took it, and they shook.

Josh felt like he was some kind of official at a formal ceremony. "So is the Will-Nav bromance back on?" he inquired, brows raised.

Will snorted. "Yeah, but only if we find another name for it."

"Yes, let us. How about the Nav-Will"—Nav struggled to find a different word but failed— "bromance?"

"Awesome. Let's celebrate!" Josh squirmed back enough to reach his pack and whipped out—what else?—the Covington House Cup. "A little more Elaine torture?"

They all laughed as they positioned themselves for yet another photo with the cup. Josh pulled out his mobile. "This one's for the books, boys!" They posed as Josh held out the cup in one hand and his phone in the other.

Click!

Nav's photo smile faded. "I say, chaps, are we actually going to sleep on the ground?"

The dining hall buzzed with chatter the next morning at breakfast. Everybody had heard that a reporter had arrived at Covington. Some students didn't know who it was yet, but Kit had told her friends. The information was crackling through the student population like a lightning bolt.

"Daisy Rooney?" Josh confirmed.

Kit nodded, but her thoughts were far away as she listened to all the buzz.

Josh, on the other hand, seemed excited. "She interviewed the Mud Slingers on their way back to London, on their tour bus! She's an awesome writer."

"I heard that she camped out all night just to get that interview," said Anya.

"And then the Foxborough Five flew her to California so she could write about their gig at the Bowl!"

Elaine happened to be walking by. "Ms. Rooney is not here to interview us because we're rock stars," she primly informed Josh as she passed.

"Speak for yourself, Elaine," he sniped.

Anya laughed. Then, looking at Kit, she asked, "Are you okay?"

Kit realized she'd been half zoned out. "Oh! Yeah. Totally. Just thinking."

At the head table, Lady Covington tapped her spoon against a glass and stood. "May I have your attention, please?"

The room quieted.

"As some of you have heard, a reporter will be joining us for a few days to do an article on Covington. Your best behavior is expected."

Kit wasn't surprised to see Elaine's hand shoot up. No matter what happened at the school, Elaine always tried to turn the attention to herself. "I've been preparing for the interview," she stated proudly. "I have information on Covington's history, the early years, the underdog victory of 1987—"

"Let us focus on the present, Elaine," Lady Covington suggested. "I would like us to share the word with potential students about what makes Covington exceptional today." She leaned forward a bit, and asked the students, "And what is our collective goal for this year?"

Everyone in the dining hall chorused, "U.K. Boarding School of the Year!" like small children in class. Kit and Anya practically sang it out, grinning at each other.

As if she'd heard Kit's thoughts, Lady Covington said, "Such good children. Sometimes, I believe we may actually attain that goal."

If we don't, poor Lady C will pop a gasket, Kit thought.

"Today we will hear your presentations," Sally told her English class.

Kit sat forward in her chair, trying to appear awake and interested. This was her first class after breakfast today, which meant that she had a big sausage, baked beans, toast with jam, fruit, and orange juice roiling around in her tummy trying to digest. Digestion always made her sleepy. She wouldn't have minded a cup of strong tea to counter it, and that made her think, *Wait, I used to like coffee more than tea! OMG, I've gone native!*

Sally was still talking. "I'm very excited to hear about all the fun things you've learned by diving into your family history. So!" She looked from student to student. "Who would like to begin?"

Elaine's hand shot into the air. Kit imagined that it made a whiplike *crack* sound, it moved so fast. And of course, nobody else volunteered. Kit considered it, but there was no way she would ace her extremely cool presentation with her eyelids drooping.

Sally gave up on anyone else and gestured at Elaine. "All right, Elaine. It looks as though you're our girl."

Shining that superior smile of hers, Elaine took her place at the front of the class. She picked up a remote control that operated the class SMART Board, declaring, "My granddad had six sisters, of which I've chosen to profile my great-aunt Dottie." She clicked the remote, and the screen showed a photo of a wealthy elderly woman wrapped in an elaborate fur coat. Elaine had placed three bullet points of information next to the photo:

- One of seven children
- Left home at sixteen
- Became a dress designer

"She was a dressmaker of some renown—" she

continued, but was interrupted when the door burst open and Daisy Rooney sailed in.

"Hi, everyone! I'm Daisy. I'm sorry I'm late. I got carried away in the dining hall. I maybe ate a thousand pastries! Is that bad?" She winked at the class.

Kit grinned, delighted to see the flashy reporter again. Daisy wore another very un-Covington-ish outfit: a black belted minidress, over-the-knee black boots (with super-high heels again, Kit noted — Daisy was rather short), and a fuzzy peach sweater. She had black nail polish on and a notebook in one hand, and she was waving her empty one around as she kept talking. "I'm sooo psyched to be here! I love your place. Bit like a castle, innit?"

"That's what I said when I got here!" Kit burst out. She found Daisy's kooky energy irresistible. *So much for sleepy digestion!* she thought, feeling totally energized again.

"Oh hey, it's Kit!" Daisy said with a wave. "Yay!"

Sally, smiling tightly, hadn't spoken so far, and Daisy suddenly seemed to realize this. She pointed to the back of the room and told Sally, "I'll sneak into the back," as if sneaking was possible after such a rowdy entrance.

Elaine cut her off. "Miss Rooney, I love your

work. I stayed up all night getting acquainted. I'm a huge fan!"

Kit rolled her eyes. Elaine was every bit the champion that she believed she was — when it came to fawning over famous people in order to get herself noticed. *If she ever meets the queen, she'll probably freak so hard, she'll turn into a puddle of goo,* Kit thought.

Daisy, however, ate it up. "Why, thank you!" she told Elaine. Then to the still-silent and rather stunned Sally, she said, "Pretend I'm not here."

Like that's possible, Kit thought in amusement.

"Really," Daisy stressed. "I just want to sink into the background and observe!"

Sally finally spoke up, looking a bit annoyed. She was, after all, *the teacher.* "Thank you. There's a seat—"

"I'll conduct one-on-one interviews over the next couple of days," Daisy went on, talking right over Sally, "and we'll see how it all shakes out!"

Kit watched Daisy pick her way down a row of chairs and then, "Oh!" Daisy squealed. She must have tripped, and she accidentally fell right into handsome Will's lap. "Soz!" she said, blushing. "I am such a pain, aren't I?"

Elaine picked up her report. "So," she began,

"Great-Aunt Dottie's gowns have been seen in society for decades, up to and including the royal court. Many have walked the red carpet—"

Another knock at the door and another interruption, this time by a student who handed Sally a message.

"Should I just hold?" Elaine asked. "Should I start from the top?"

Sally was reading the message. "Will," she said, "Lady Covington would like to see you in her office."

Will grabbed his backpack, and as he went past her, Kit saw the look of complete mystery on his face. Whatever Lady Covington wanted, it was a surprise to Will.

When Will entered the headmistress's office, the last person he expected to see was seated by the desk: his father. Rudy was present as well. Dreading the next ten minutes, Will took the seat next to his father and waited.

"Mr. Palmerston," began Lady Covington.

"Yes, ma'am?" said Will's father.

Showing only the slightest trace of amusement,

Lady Covington told the older man, "I was speaking to your son."

If it had been anybody else's father, Will would have laughed like crazy at the mistake. He loved when adults messed up their dignified conversations. But as it was, he didn't even smile. He felt like crawling away. . . .

"Mr. Palmerston-*the-younger*," Lady Covington began again, "you have managed to fall behind in every single subject."

"He's got an A in Equestrian," Rudy interjected.

Will thought it was extremely kind of Rudy to say so, but he knew it wouldn't make any difference. If this meeting was about his grades and his dad was present, Will knew he was doomed.

"Without academic excellence—"

"We will do whatever it takes to compensate for Will's academic weaknesses," Mr. Palmerston-the-elder cut in.

"Will's not a bad kid," Rudy added. "And he's our best rider."

Lady Covington said sharply, "Mr. Bridges, you are here as William's adviser. I will ask you if your advice is required."

Will was good at holding in anger. Otherwise he would have stood up for his teacher. Rudy was the only adult in a hundred-mile radius who had ever stood up for *him*. But again, he did nothing—except inwardly shudder as his father spoke once more. Will hated the way his father spoke, always using that snobby tone designed to make his listeners feel inferior, always pushing his own desires like nobody else mattered.

"There must be a solution," Mr. Palmerston insisted. "This is the best place for him."

Lady Covington nodded but said, "There have also been incidents where Will's behavior has been less than exemplary."

"We have to get this sorted. I can't have him at home. I just can't." Mr. Palmerston glanced at Will. "Not now."

Will didn't want to meet his father's eyes, but he couldn't stop himself. It was like leaning far over a cliff, knowing he would fall but doing it anyway. His father didn't want him, his mother didn't want him, and now Covington didn't want him. When that was reality, what was the point of *anything*?

His father eyes seemed dead. There was no

warmth in his expression, none at all. "You don't want to live with the baby," the man said. "And Tanya's expecting another. We told you that you couldn't muck everything up again, not here. Do you know how much it cost me the last time you pulled this nonsense?"

Lady Covington did not speak right away. Will saw her exchange a glance with Rudy, and then she straightened some papers, thinking. "A letter of probation will be issued immediately," she finally said. "William may stay through the term exams, but we will need to see a substantial improvement, or we will have to expel him."

Will sat like a statue, waiting for someone to tell him he could leave. Stay, leave, jump up and down and scream — what did it all matter, anyway?

Chapter 10

OFF THE RECORD

Much to her surprise, Kit's classmates presentations were actually turning out to be fun. Elaine's dress-designing great-aunt Dottie had led a more interesting life than Kit had first suspected. And after Elaine, Alistair Pring talked about his great-great-grandfather who had been associated with the early Zoological Society of London. In 1826, he had helped establish the London Zoo!

Kiki Welch then discussed her great-grandfather who had worked as a clerk for archaeologist Howard Carter during his 1923 excavation of the tomb of King Tutankhamen — King Tut! She showed them a jar of sand from Tut's tomb that had been passed down to her. How cool was that?

Kit thought Kiki's story couldn't be beat until Anya made her presentation. Anya bravely chose to talk about her royal family. Kit saw how hard it was for her, but when nobody made a big deal out of it, Anya relaxed and began to enjoy herself. She started by explaining that a maharaja was a king or prince in India. She then talked about past maharajas in her family, especially one who had "insisted on sleeping in a tree house. He didn't set foot inside that palace! So I come from a long line of rebels. Brave little rebels." She clicked the remote to show a closer view of the tree house in question.

According to bullet points next to the picture, the tree house had had six servants, gold-plated toilets, an aviary, an organic herb garden, and a swimming pond filled with goat's milk. *Wow, I'd live in that!* Kit thought. *Except I'd avoid the goat milk pool. Eww.*

Anya went on: "Okay, so the tree house was pretty lavish—I'm not going to lie. . . ."

Then Nav told them about his great-great-grandfather General Andrada. "It is said that my grandfather's grandfather took down an entire army with nothing but"—he paused dramatically, his eyes flashing—"a pocketknife!" He displayed a map that showed where General Andrada's ship had been ambushed, where he had fought the army single-handedly, and where the legendary pocketknife had been lost at sea.

Kit wondered if he was fibbing. *I mean, really, just a pocketknife?*

Josh came next. "My great-grandparents were maple syrup farmers," he announced. "And if any-body's going to make a joke about that, I'm just going to sic Nav's grandfather on them."

Class was almost over, so Kit volunteered next. She didn't want to wait until the following day, plus everybody else's presentations had gotten her all revved up. "So, uh. Wow," she said as she stood before the class clutching the SMART Board remote. "Those are hard acts to follow."

That was when her dad sneaked into class and slipped to the back of the room. He'd come to hear her presentation!

Kit gave him a wave and continued. "I really wanted to dive into my mom's side of the family, but it was really weird. The town she said she was from, Westingate? It doesn't actually exist, and it was a total dead end. But . . ." She clicked the remote, and the SMART Board showed a photo of a young man in the

Old West, only he was wearing a top hat instead of a cowboy hat. Next to the photo were the words:

BILLY THE KID
MYTH, LEGEND, FAMILY?
by Katherine Bridges

"I found out that my dad comes by his cowboy-ness quite honestly, because the Bridges are related to Billy the Kid!"

"Billy the Kit?" Anya asked, confused. "Is that who they named you after?"

Kit looked out at her classmates. All of them wore expressions of equal confusion. "Billy the *Kid*," she repeated, enunciating very clearly.

Blank stares.

"Guys, c'mon!"

Crickets.

"He was only one of the wildest outlaws of the Wild West!" Kit said, and she clicked the remote, revealing another picture of Billy under the heading *Cowboyness*. "William H. Bonney was his real name," she said, "and he raced horses, and stole horses, and then he had his own horse stolen *from* him. And listen, do I ever feel for old Billy on that one."

She paused. That was the worst thing she could

have said, because instantly her thoughts turned to TK. When Daisy mouthed *What?* from her seat at the back of the room, Kit automatically explained. "I mean TK, even though he's a horse, belongs on my family tree. He is family. He . . . he totally got me. And now . . . he's gone. . . ." Emotions started to bubble up. Kit blinked back moisture in her eyes. "He was a really special horse, you know? And maybe these feelings are because I come from a long line of horse people."

Daisy appeared to be very interested in this TK story, but Kit couldn't seem to talk anymore when she noticed her father's face. He wore a sad smile, and Kit knew that he cared more about her loss than he let on. The problem was, it didn't seem like he could do anything about it.

Kit turned helplessly to Sally and held out the remote. She hadn't gotten very far, but her presentation was over.

Will left Lady Covington's office feeling like he was nothing. That's how his father always made him feel—like he didn't exist. No, wait. That wasn't quite right. His father definitely made him feel like he existed, but without any value. He made Will feel like a sharp rock in the road, something that caused problems for everyone traveling through life, something that should be kicked aside, out of the way, out of sight.

Something that his father—probably everybody—would prefer gone.

"Will!"

He didn't want to talk to anyone, but he couldn't very well ignore his teacher. He slowed down as Sally hurried over. She matched his stride, saying, "I'm so sorry you missed the presentations."

"Yeah."

"Shall we schedule you for tomorrow? There are still a few—"

"Mine's not done," Will told her flatly.

"Oh," Sally said. "It's not?"

"Didn't have time." He walked faster and was glad when Sally let him go. After he turned the corner, he pulled his finished report out of his backpack.

He threw it into the trash bin.

Elaine was thrilled to see Daisy in the dining hall at lunchtime. And the reporter was conducting interviews! Right now, Jilly Jones was her subject, so Elaine decided to make sure *she* was next.

She hurriedly fetched a cup of tea—she would appear much more adult with tea instead of a sandwich—then surveyed the scene. Jilly was sitting on one side of Daisy, so Elaine snagged the seat on Daisy's other side. "Ms. Rooney," she said, lightly touching the reporter's arm. "What luck! You're doing interviews?"

Daisy threw her a *duh* look. "Just a mo, yeah?" She resumed talking to Jilly.

Basking in self-confidence, Elaine straightened her collar and arranged her cup of tea just so, presuming that Daisy would take a photo. Elaine was sure that once the reporter heard about all of her incredible accomplishments, she would become the focus of the article. She was the perfect Covington student, after all, the ultimate example of what Lady Covington liked to call "the Covington ideal." That's what the article was supposed to do, right? Lure ideal candidates to the school?

When Jilly stood up to leave, Elaine leaned toward Daisy. "I'm ready, Ms. Rooney."

Daisy turned to face Elaine. "And you are?"

It surprised Elaine that the reporter wouldn't know who she was. Oh, well, she would remedy that. "I'm Elaine Whiltshire, Fourth Form, and best rider at Covington." She then proceeded to rattle off details of her academic grades and equestrian achievements, never noticing that Daisy wasn't taking notes. Or taking photos. Or taking much of an interest, really. "And I live to help other students," Elaine enthused once she'd finished her litany of personal stats. "I mean, this term has been challenging in terms of workload, but I manage. And I'm assigned to train Kit, who insisted on riding this crazy horse—"

"Okay!" Daisy said, glancing up from her mobile. "Thanks a bunch! I'm going to grab something to eat."

"But we haven't talked about my goals and ambitions yet," Elaine pointed out.

Daisy closed her notebook. "Oh, we have loads of time," she said as she left.

Elaine grinned. Of course there was more time. She went to the buffet table, chose a sandwich, ate it quickly, and then headed to her room. She had a plan. . . .

Kit was just stuffing two juicy strawberries and a hunk of melon into her mouth when she heard Daisy's distinct voice. "Mind if I join you?"

Kit nodded, struggling to chew.

"I have to say," Daisy began, sitting down, "you totally remind me of myself. When I was thirteen, my parents moved to Paris and chucked me into boarding school. Imagine how I stuck out!"

Kit chewed and swallowed down the last of the fruit. "Oh, I feel you. There's royalty here. Diplomats' kids, heirs to massive fortunes, and then — there's me."

"Elaine seems like a good friend."

"She's the best rider in the school. That's why she's my tutor, if by tutor you mean *drill sergeant*. Totally type A."

Daisy flashed a wicked grin. "Bit of a monster, then?"

Kit grinned back. "A bit!"

They shared a laugh, and Kit found herself liking Daisy more and more. She was so easy to talk to!

"She doesn't seem like a big fan of TK," Daisy said next.

Kit slumped. "TK was the best horse. He and I

turned dangerous and unpredictable into quirky and particular!"

Will walked by, and Kit gave him a smile. He did not smile back. His face seemed frozen in a frown. *I wonder what happened in Lady C's office*, Kit thought. *Can't have been good. . . .*

"Dish!" Daisy whispered at her, one eyebrow raised in interest as she watched Will's retreating back.

"Oh, it's nothing."

"You know who I looked at like that? Danny McCabe." Daisy shook her shoulders with a "Woo! Total rugby fanatic. He had this crazy mop of blond curls that flopped into his eyes. Dreamy!"

Kit had nothing to say to that as she tore her eyes away from Will. They landed on Nav, sitting nearby, and he gave her a cheery wave.

"Or is it that one?" Daisy said, openly fishing for romance gossip. "Spill, Kit!"

"Oh, come on," Kit said. "I was just . . . looking at the pastries."

Daisy cocked her head. She didn't look like she believed Kit any more than Kit did herself. They both laughed.

"Oh," came an all-too-familiar voice. "Is this seat empty?"

Kit almost lost her lunch. There stood Elaine, blinking innocently at Daisy while one hand lay lightly on the back of an empty chair and the other hand — well, the whole arm was holding a bunch of big ruffled show rosettes with colorful ribbons trailing down.

It must have taken her a while to arrange all those so they didn't overlap, Kit thought, laughing hysterically inside. On the outside, though, she said with calm interest, "Nice ribbons, Elaine."

"Oh, these?" Elaine pretended to suddenly notice them. "These are just some awards I won last year."

Seeing Daisy's look of disgust, Kit pressed Elaine further. "And *why* are you carrying them around . . . ?"

Elaine just giggled.

She's stalling for time to try to think of something clever to say, and she can't do it! Kit thought, highly entertained. *She could make a TV series, the* I Want Attention Show! *Elaine would be a hit!*

Elaine fiddled with one of the ribbons. She appeared to still be thinking, but she seemed to come up empty. She flashed a forced model's smile at Daisy and made an awkward exit.

Kit and Daisy enjoyed a good laugh.

Later in Juniper Cottage, Nav was trying to close an important deal with Leo Ducasse.

"I will tell you where the horse is, but only if I get Josh back as my roommate," Leo said as he walked with Nav down the hallway. Leo took a bite out of a lumpy chocolate bar and chewed it in what seemed an anxious manner.

Nav couldn't stand the smell of cheap milk chocolate. Dark chocolate, very dark chocolate, was the only decent form, in his opinion. But chocolate preferences aside, he wanted to know only one thing from Leo. "Are you sure this information is correct?"

"To the best of my knowledge," Leo replied, chewing. "I told you, it pays to have famous friends. People talk."

Nav still couldn't understand Leo's point of view. "Do you really like rooming with Josh that much?" he asked. "I personally find him rather annoying."

"No, I love him!" Leo enthused in his strong French accent. "Did you know he can bake?" Leo's smile disappeared. "But it's mainly that I can't stand another second of Will's titanic mess. You have got to save me! Thanks to William, I am living on Mount Trash!" Leo held up a slip of paper.

Josh eyed it. "Hand it over."

"Only if we have a deal."

With a nod, Nav plucked the paper from Leo's fingers. "We have a deal."

That night after dinner, Kit was on her way to her room when Daisy appeared. "Finally!" the reporter said, heaving a sigh. "I've been looking everywhere for you."

"For me?" Kit asked.

"Yeah," said Daisy. "We're not done talking yet, are we? I've heard about so much going on around here, and I think you"—she pointed at Kit—"can help me sort it all out, yeah?" She added with a wink, "Got a lot in common, you and me. Like good mates. Makes it easier, you know?"

Kit felt like she'd been given a high compliment. *Daisy is famous, and she considers me a friend, somebody who can help her? Wow!* "Sure, come on," Kit said, and she headed for the staircase.

"So tell me about that totally cute guy from

lunchtime," Daisy said. "The first one, Mr. Serious. If you ask me, he belongs on a magazine cover."

"Tell me about it," Kit agreed. "His name is Will Palmerston. He's really nice when you get to know him. He just doesn't talk much. He really helped me, too. He's a great rider. Fearless, the kind that belongs with the horses."

"And the other one? The smooth one?"

They were *all* smooth, as far as Kit could tell. "There are lots of sophisticated boys here from all over the world. Totally crush-worthy!" She said that last part in a low voice. It wasn't that she didn't want to tell Daisy that particular juicy truth. She simply didn't want everybody else to hear her say it.

Daisy said, "He seems really nice, too."

"And smart. And charming."

When they reached Kit's room, Daisy stopped dead in the doorway. "Wow! This bedroom is fab! Way better than my boarding school. We were jammed in six to a bedroom. It was like living in a shoe box!" She wandered in, looking around, and then zeroed in on Kit's bed. With a leap, she flung herself on the soft mattress. *Whomp!*

Kit laughed, remembering how she'd done the

exact same thing the day she'd arrived at Covington. "Now that we're here," she said, "do we start the slumber party?"

Daisy perched herself on Anya's bed. "Let's make it interesting. Truth or Dare. Which boy does your heart really belong to? I'm dying to know."

"So not fair!" Kit responded.

"Well, tell me anyway."

Kit debated between Will then Nav then Will then Nav—and then blurted out, "TK." When Daisy rolled her eyes, Kit said, "I really love him. Call me a cheeseball, but we conquered our fears together, and that leaves you bonded for life, you know?"

Daisy nodded, listening.

"Hey, wait," Kit said as a terrific idea came to her. "Do you have ways we might be able to find TK?" Surely if anybody could track down a missing person (or horse), it would be a reporter.

"I could totally look into it," Daisy offered. "But how did you lose him?"

Anya entered the room in workout sweats with her iPod in her hand. She gave Kit a smile in greeting as she removed her earbuds.

Kit waved back. "He and I basically embarrassed

Lady C by not being perfect, so she sent him away," she said to Daisy.

"She didn't!"

"She did. It's just the worst. It's all rules, all the time."

Daisy sat up very straight and said as if she were Lady Covington, "Young lady, it has come to my attention that you had corn puffs for breakfast when the rules strictly state that Wednesday is an oatmeal day."

Kit joined in. "Katherine Bridges, detention for life!"

Daisy laughed, but behind her, Anya seemed upset. She stared pointedly at Kit.

Clueless, Kit smiled back as Daisy said, "I can't believe she sent TK away."

"I'm going to find him," Kit stated. "And bring him back. Print that, would you?"

Now Anya looked positively alarmed. "Kit!" she said sharply. "Curfew?" She indicated Daisy.

Kit didn't know exactly what time it was, but it certainly wasn't late enough for curfew. "No, it's not," she said, "not until—"

"Curfew!" Anya insisted.

Kit noticed Daisy's amusement. "You're a

trip, Kit," the reporter said. "Shall we chat more tomorrow?"

"I would love that!" Kit replied happily. What a hoot! She was making friends with a famous reporter! She couldn't stop grinning after Daisy left.

Anya wasn't grinning, not one bit. "So much gossip!" she said, aghast. "Just please tell me you said the three magic words?"

Whoa, what's the matter? Kit thought. Anya's frown had a hard edge to it that Kit had never seen before. *Okay, maybe she doesn't like Daisy. Or maybe she doesn't like reporters?* Either way, Kit could only guess what Anya's three magic words might be. "Abracadabra? Ta-da? Hocus-pocus?"

"Off the record," Anya stated. "You do realize she could print everything you just said. And she probably will!"

"Daisy wouldn't do that."

"It's something I learned in princess training. Don't tell the media anything you don't want to see on a billboard."

Kit's heart sank. *Uh-oh.*

Chapter 11

ANYTHING
FOR A FRIEND

At her father's request, Kit began the next morning in the tack room with him and a cup of yummy hot chocolate. She was mostly getting used to the damp English mornings, but despite her layered school uniform, her hands were always cold. It was wonderful to hold the hot cup and feel a thousand tiny tendrils of warmth seep through her fingers.

"So the reporter was fun?" Rudy asked her, leaning back in his chair and thudding one booted foot down on the tabletop.

Kit slurped some of her drink, smacking her lips in approval. "She had a million hilarious stories about the bands that she's interviewed, but . . . I may have pulled a bit of a Kit." Long ago the phrase "pulling a

Kit" had become code for blabbering on without an end in sight.

"What, did you say something that wasn't quite true?" Rudy asked.

"I mostly talked about TK . . . ?"

"Oh, I wouldn't worry about it too much."

"I hope I don't have to. So what's up? Why did you ask me to meet you before class?"

Rudy set down his cocoa and stood. "I wanted to give you something," he explained, heading for the shelf unit against the opposite wall. "I saw your presentation yesterday, and I can tell it's been bugging you." He picked up a polished wooden box and carried it over to Kit. "Before we moved, I put a few of your mom's things together just in case either of us got to missing her too much. I was waiting for the right time to give it to you."

Kit braced herself before lifting the lid. The box wasn't very big, but she was sure that whatever Rudy had chosen to put into it would make her cry. *Heck,* she thought, *I almost cried at the House Cup when he gave me mom's lucky Ugly Brooch, and that brooch is the grossest thing on the planet!* Kit still had it, though, safely stored in her room.

She slowly lifted the box lid. Memories flooded her mind at the sight of the first item, a small plush horse. Kit remembered giving it to her mom as a birthday present when she had been five years old. It had been one of those presents a kid gives a parent because they're the one who really wants it. Rudy had helped her pick it out, of course.

"What shall I name such a pretty little horse?" Elizabeth had asked young Kit.

Kit had been in love with a TV show about a girl and her pony called Moony, so she had replied, "Moony!"

Now Kit picked Moony up and set him aside, fighting off tears. Underneath Moony lay Dabney the Dragon, a green hand puppet her mother had used to play "doctor" whenever Kit had gotten sick. Dabney, her mom had explained, specialized in "sick Kits," so he was always the one who brought her frosty Popsicles when she had a sore throat or tissues when she had a cold. Now, without her mom's graceful fingers guiding his movements, Dabney looked less like a doctor and more like a patient.

Oh, there were so many wonderful mementos in the box! But suddenly, all Kit could think about were the things that *weren't* there, like the answers to several mysterious questions. "It just doesn't make any sense," she said. "When I was little, we invented this whole town made out of old cans and boxes, remember? And we called it Westingate because that's where she came from."

"You're right," said Rudy. "I remember that."

"What does it mean?"

Rudy shrugged helplessly. "I don't know. I just know that her parents died when she was seventeen, and she moved to the States. She never wanted to talk about it more than that."

"I thought you lovebirds told each other everything," Kit teased, waggling her eyebrows.

Rudy smiled. "Except that. She always said it made her too sad to think about. I didn't want to push her. Maybe this"—and Rudy knocked on the box with one knuckle—"will help you figure some things out."

Maybe, Kit thought. *I hope so.*

After his meeting with Leo, Nav looked for Josh and found him out on the grounds watching a rugby match between the boys of Birch House and Alder House. "If you have a moment, I would like to speak with you," he told Josh.

"Sure, roomie. I gotta get back for class anyway."

So the two boys walked together. Nav chatted aimlessly for a few minutes about horses and whatnot, trying to lull Josh into a false sense of security before he pounced on the real issue: "Joshua, we need to solve our dorm-room difficulty. You know things can't stay the way they are."

"Difficulty?" Josh asked. "What difficulty? Look, it's a done deal. I mean, why would I want to switch again? My hearing is only just coming back."

Nav presumed he was referring to Leo, and his jackhammer snoring. Unfortunately for Josh, facts like snoring didn't matter, not to Nav, anyway. *"Les jeux sont faits,"* he said in French. "The game is over. You simply *must* move out of my room now."

Josh shook his head. "No way, dude. Absolutely not, okay? It's never going to happen."

"Okay, look. Name your price for the room. I will entertain all offers until noon. After that, you leave me no choice but to employ the Too Bad Clause."

"What's that?"

Nav did his best to translate "You'll find out" into a facial expression. He let Josh get nice and nervous before turning his back and leaving.

Kit munched cereal in the dining hall while picking through the memory box Rudy had given her. Along with Moony the plush horse and Dabney the dragon puppet, she found the ribbon her mother had won at the Fox Run Horse Show. The event had been a fund-raiser for the Fox Run Horse Club for Kids, which Kit had joined when she was eight—right before her accident with Freckles.

Her mom had entered the Parents' Pony Run, a hysterical event involving ponies, fistfuls of juicy carrots, and lots of silly running around. Elizabeth Bridges had maintained the family's honor and won first place. Kit remembered laughing so hard that she'd almost tossed her picnic lunch.

I miss you, Mom, she thought, closing the box. Then she spotted the person she'd hoped to see most since the evening before. "Daisy!" she called.

"Hi!" said Daisy, coming over.

The flamboyant reporter wasn't dressed quite as loudly as the day before. She still sported a miniskirt and those wild boots, but today she wore a simple white knit top. Her sweater, on the other hand, might have been made out of a fuzzy yak. "I'm so glad I ran into you," Kit said.

"Well, it's nice to see you, too," Daisy said, taking a seat.

"Yeah. So, um, yesterday, I, uh, well—I kind of have a big mouth, and I said all sorts of things, but I sort of forgot the three most important words."

Daisy leaned in and suggested, "*I love crisps?* No, wait—*he's so cute!*"

Kit shook her head. "Off the record." She expected Daisy to get upset.

If anything, Daisy seemed charmed by Kit's nervousness. "Oh, Kit, you're so cute. Don't worry. I don't even know what the main focus of the story is yet or who it's going to be about. And I was thinking, if I do write about TK, it could be a really big help in finding him."

Was she serious? Would she really go out of her way like that to help? "That would be awesome! Thank you!" The tight lump of fear in Kit's chest loosened, and she sat back, relieved. "Phew! 'Cause sometimes I shoot my mouth off and—"

"Don't give it another thought." With that settled,

Daisy pointed at the memory box. "What's happening here?"

"Oh," Kit said, opening the box again, "check this out. I told you that stuff about my mom? Well, my dad gave me this box of her old things. He thought it might help solve the mystery."

Daisy peered inside. Instantly her eyebrows shot up. "Oh, crazy coincidence!" She picked up an old all-access pass for a band called Box of Kittens, appearing at the Glacier Club, in London, on their "Adorable Tour." "I know the bass player from Box of Kittens, Rupert Jackson. He was one of my first ever interviews, and we kept in touch."

"Really?"

"Yeah. Do you think your mum was in the music scene?"

Knowing so little about her mother's past made that a difficult question to answer. "She knew her music," Kit said, remembering her mom's collection of CDs, cassettes, and old vinyl albums. "But she was only in London a little bit before she moved overseas."

"I can ask him, if you like," Daisy offered. "Can't hurt. I'll take a snap!" She used her mobile to take a photo of the badge. "You look like her."

"You think so?" Kit fidgeted in her chair, recalling times when she'd stood in front of her bedroom mirror with a photo of her mom, wondering if they looked anything alike. She'd never thought so, and that had always made her feel strange. But here was Daisy, telling her there was a resemblance. "I'd like that," Kit said, smiling.

Daisy poked at her mobile. "I'll text this to Rupert and see if he recognizes her from the old Box of Kittens days."

"You'd do that for me?"

Daisy smiled. "Anything for a friend."

After dinner, Will couldn't face going back to his room, soon to be filled by Leo's thunderous snoring, so he went to the stable. It was as good a time as any to clean Wayne's stall. When he was done with that, he gave the chestnut gelding a good grooming.

While he worked, he entertained Wayne with a complete report of the day's events. He liked to keep Wayne up to date, but today he really needed to unload. Who else could he talk to?

"It's boring," he grumbled while brushing Wayne's silky coat. "And it's irrelevant. Like, when am I actually going to need maths in the real world?"

Wayne grunted and lipped some hay into his mouth. He nudged Will, chewing, as if to say, "Well, go on."

Will resumed brushing. "My dad would say I need it so I don't end up living in some alley somewhere. But like he and the dread Tanya even care, as long as it's not their alley."

He froze as a crash sounded outside of Wayne's stall. "Oh, no!" squeaked a familiar voice.

Kit wanted to kick herself. She had come to the stables to visit TK's stall.

No, not visit. If she was going to be honest, she had planned to *brood* in TK's stall. Again. But when she'd heard Will talking to Wayne, she'd gotten curious. *Stupid shovels*, she thought of the stack she'd just knocked over. She straightened up so that she could peek through the bars of Wayne's stall and see Will.

Will saw her, too.

"I am so sorry," Kit said, carefully stepping out of the pile of fallen shovels. "I was trying to make a graceful exit to give you some space, but I'm me, so grace isn't exactly my go-to. Knocking a bunch of shovels over, though? That's totally my specialty."

Will set down the soft body brush he'd been using on Wayne and joined her outside the stall. He folded his arms but said nothing.

"It helps, though, doesn't it? Talking to them?" Kit watched Will glance at Wayne, who blinked back at him, lazily chewing his hay. She imagined TK doing that and remembered how she would lose herself in his bright brown eyes. "I really miss TK. Just being near his stall sometimes helps." Then she realized what her presence must have looked like to Will. "And that's what I was doing, I swear! I wasn't eavesdropping."

Will gave her a knowing smirk.

"They're great listeners," Kit went on. "And so am I. Actually. So if you want to talk—"

"No," Will muttered, shaking his head. "I don't know. . . ."

He seemed so sad that Kit couldn't help but try to lift his spirits. "I know," she said apologetically. "I'm no Wayne."

That made Will chuckle.

Score one for Bridges! Kit thought, pleased with herself. "So you got to see your dad today?"

"Yeah. For fifteen minutes. He drove two hours here to make me feel awful."

"Just for fifteen minutes?"

"Yeah. Lady Covington wanted a meeting. So she spoke through most of the fifteen minutes anyway."

"Sounds like her. It's too bad he didn't get to stay to hear your family tree project. Who'd you do?"

"Him." Will smiled, a bitter smile that made Kit's heart go out to him. "He used to be my favorite person."

Kit debated how to respond. She had no idea what it would feel like to have uncaring parents. Being rejected by anybody hurt badly enough, but your own parents?

Dual rings broke the conversation. Kit and Will both pulled out their mobiles. Kit's screen displayed a text message: *Please come to the student lounge as soon as possible. Thank you. Nav.*

Kit had gotten texts from Nav before and always laughed at his lack of abbreviations. Then again, he was always so smart and proper that spelling everything out in full and using proper punctuation was probably part of Navarro DNA.

Will showed her that he'd received the same message. "Just before venturing into potentially awkward territory full of *the feels*," he said with a small grin. "Come on, let's go."

When Kit and Will arrived in the student lounge a few minutes later, the first thing to greet their eyes was a bed, or more specifically, bedclothes. Josh's sheets, blankets, and pillows lay arranged on the floor as though they were on an actual bed. Boxes stuffed with Josh's belongings were stacked on either side. Next to them, an umbrella stand had been loaded with a hockey stick, baseball bat, golf clubs, and various pairs of athletic shoes.

Nav flashed his most suave smile in greeting. "Wait for it," he instructed in a mysterious tone.

Kit wanted to ask what was going on when Josh ran in, followed by Anya. "What is this?" he demanded when he saw his stuff all over the floor.

"This, my friend, is the Too Bad Clause," Nav practically sang at him. "As in too bad you didn't listen to me, because I would have offered a myriad of perks had you simply moved out as requested. Instead"—he waved at all the stuff like a game show host revealing a prize—"welcome to your new accommodations!"

Josh wasn't happy. "You can't do this! I mean, who put you in charge, out of all people?" He turned to Will for help, and Kit found herself actually feeling sorry for him. She knew about the big roommate switcheroo, though she didn't know details. She did, however, know that everybody had ended up unhappy about it except for Josh. "Come on, dude," Josh said to Will. "A bet's a bet, right?" He was practically pleading, but Will merely shrugged at him.

Elaine sat at a nearby table working on her laptop. "This is a study area," she stated, "not a personal playground. Besides, you're all completely daft."

"What's she talking about?" Josh demanded, frazzled.

Nav gestured at Elaine as if to say *Go on*, and she quoted from memory, "'For health and safety reasons, no student is to leave their assigned room. There are to be no exceptions.' Covington rule book, page forty-six, regulation five hundred and two A."

Even Josh couldn't work a way around that. Defeated, he asked, "Can I at least get some help?"

Kit stepped forward first, followed by Anya.

"Thank you," Josh told them, and they got to work gathering his belongings.

Will had no interest in helping Josh. True, he was the one who had started this whole roommate merry-go-round, but he felt no responsibility for how much Josh had rubbed Nav's nose in it. Besides, now Will could go back to the nice big room with Nav and leave Josh to Leo "Snores-Like-a-Construction-Site" Ducasse.

He sat down by Elaine. "Hey. You writing an article?" He'd noticed her laptop screen. It showed a photo of Elaine, next to which a headline read "Life at The Covington Academy with Elaine Whiltshire."

"Despite my best efforts, Ms. Rooney didn't seem to find me as interesting as she did Kit," Elaine admitted.

Will was aware of Elaine's resentment for all the attention that Kit drew. Personally, he didn't care what the world thought about him, but he knew how much Elaine valued what she referred to as her "public face." He said to her, "You don't have to be in an article to be interesting."

"Easy for you to say."

"But it's true."

"I'm trying to get my portfolio together for my Oxford application. Being featured in an article would have really helped and yet . . ."

Will knew that getting into Oxford was Elaine's ultimate life goal. Everything she did, from volunteering for the smallest bake sale to riding in the biggest competition—all of it had been carefully plotted out by her and her parents to help her get into Oxford.

Will could not relate to that. As much as he knew that he should prepare for his future, his parents had never helped him make plans. They didn't care what he did, as long as he did it well, upheld the family name, and didn't bother them. So Will had gravitated to what interested him the most—horses. But making a "horse plan"? He didn't know how to make one of those, or any other kind of plan. Nobody had ever shown him how to do that.

No wonder his academics were horrid.

Shaking off his thoughts, he stood up. "You've got plenty to offer as you are," he told Elaine, and he tapped the Close button on her laptop. The faux article vanished.

As he sauntered away, Elaine called out, "Thank you, Will."

Will called back, "G'night, Whiltshire."

When Kit and Anya finished helping poor Josh settle back into his side of the room with Leo, they decided to go to Rose Cottage and get some studying done. The second Anya saw Kit's memory box, however, she had to see what was inside.

The girls sat on the window seat and pawed through photos and knickknacks, but they kept going back to the Box of Kittens concert badge.

"Maybe your mom traveled all around going to music festivals," suggested Anya.

Kit was shuffling through photographs her mother had taken when she was young. "She liked to take pictures. Maybe she was a photographer for some huge band or something."

"Maybe she was *in* the band!" Anya said.

Kit imagined how cool that would be. If it were true, though, what could possibly have made her mother stop? And why keep it a secret? Kit might have grown up with Garth Brooks as a family friend or something!

She was about to voice this thought when some-one rapped on the door. Daisy sailed in. "I've just come to say bye," the reporter said cheerfully. "You, my darling," she aimed at Kit, "have been soooo helpful."

Kit grinned, though she noticed how Anya frowned. Kit understood Anya's dislike of Daisy now, but she still hoped that the reporter might help find TK. "Good," she told Daisy. "Great!"

"Okay, then!" Daisy said, giving Kit a quick hug. "I'm off! *Ciao!*"

She was almost out the door when Kit managed to blurt out, "Wait! Daisy!"

Daisy turned around.

"Did you find out anything?"

"About . . . ?"

"The stuff you promised to look into for me? My mom? My horse? Anything . . . ?"

Daisy adopted an expression of total innocence.

Kit got desperate. "I really need this information, because I can't find out anything about either of them!"

"Right. Well," Daisy said, "Rupert didn't know your mum at all. And, um, I'll try and work the horse thing into the article, okay?"

Kit had always heard the phrase "to have the rug jerked out from under you." Now she knew what it meant. "You promised," she said in a small voice.

"No, luv," Daisy corrected her. "I promised to try. Ta-ta, then!"

Daisy was gone, and so were Kit's hopes. She sank down on the couch, crestfallen.

Suddenly Dabney the dragon appeared next to her and said in a high squeaky voice, "I'm sorry."

Kit tried to smile but failed.

Anya pulled the Dabney puppet off her hand and knelt down next to Kit. "I know you were counting on that."

"I just don't get it. Nothing makes sense anymore. I thought this would bring me closer to my mom, but now I feel further away from her than ever."

Kit reached out her toe to kick the box closed.

Chapter 12

SECRET PLANS

The next morning, Kit and Anya walked to class together under a perfect blue sky. A light breeze carried the scent of moist earth and grass, and birds cheeped and twittered pleasantly. It was the kind of morning that usually filled Kit's heart with joyful expectation.

But not this time.

"Maybe we could go to the village later for a little outing," Anya suggested as they walked arm in arm.

"Yeah." Kit sighed. "I don't know."

"Or we could beg the cook to let us make one of those ice-cream Saturday things. Is that what they're called?"

"Maybe," Kit said, distracted.

When they reached the steps leading up to the main building, they ran into Nav and Josh. "Good morning," Nav greeted them. To Kit, he said, "May I borrow you for a moment?"

"Sure," Kit said numbly. She followed Nav to a spot under a shady oak tree and waited, her brain feeling dull, her thoughts pointless.

Nav beamed at her. "I have news for you, and I think it will make you very happy."

"Good luck with that. I'm not in a great mood today."

"Well, that's about to change."

Kit tried to rally some enthusiasm. Whatever Nav wanted to say obviously held great meaning for him. She felt like a big waste of cosmic space, but she didn't want to make him feel that way, too. "Okay, so try me," she said, forcing a smile.

"I didn't tell you last night because I wasn't sure," Nav began. "But now I'm quite certain." He paused. "I've found TK!"

Kit's entire body reacted in one split second. Her heart raced, her skin prickled, her thoughts grew sharp as tacks, and her hopelessness vanished. "Are you serious?" she squealed.

Kit and Nav speed-walked into English class and made it to their seats just as class officially began. "Right to the wire," Sally noted sternly, but she let it go at that. "Good morning, all," she told the whole class. "The first topic today is surely going to be your very favorite—the upcoming midterm examinations!" She began to write on the blackboard.

Kit immediately turned around and whispered to Nav behind her, "You're sure? You're sure that it's TK? *My* TK?"

"I'm quite sure. But for now, you have to try to keep the information secret. We cannot have Lady Covington alerted."

"What do we do next? How do we get to France?"

"TK is not in France. My information puts him in the next county."

"He's here? Lady Covington lied about where she sent him?"

"It seems a feasible explanation."

"Do the two of you have something to say on the matter?"

Kit about-faced to find Sally looking down her

nose at her. Sally rarely became angry in class (or ever, really), but the subject of midterm exams were, Kit knew, highly important. Sally was not happy with their whisperings.

Like a knight riding to the rescue, Nav diverted Sally's attention away from Kit and onto himself. "Your midterm review schedule is perfect, Miss Warrington," he gushed. "I'm sure we will all succeed. We could hardly fail after all your diligent work."

That's laying it on a little thick, Kit thought, but it worked. Sally looked like she was trying not to smile, but Kit could see that Nav's absurdly bloated praise clearly tickled her—especially since she hadn't yet written the schedule down. Kit saw the chalk in her hand, but the chalkboard was blank except for one word: MIDTERM. *Oops,* she thought.

"Thank you, Nav" was all Sally said to him. To the class, she continued, "These handouts will remind you which authors we will be reviewing." She gestured for everyone to come take a handout.

As students got up and meandered to the front, Kit spun back around, saying to Nav, "One county over? What are we still doing here?"

"We need a solid plan," Nav insisted. "Tomorrow's

Saturday. It should be easier to slip away. Could we ask your father if—?"

"No. He's not a big fan of me finding TK. I maybe brought that on myself with the whole running-away-to-London biz. . . ."

"We will have to find our own way, then. Are you up for an adventure tomorrow?"

Did he need to ask? "Always," she said. She was always ready for TK. She was so excited, she could hardly stand it. "I'm going to find my horse!"

Anya was worried about Kit. Nav had taken her away earlier to deliver some kind of secret message, and Anya hadn't had a chance to talk with her since.

"We need to do something for her," she told Josh. She'd come to the tuckshop to buy Kit a candy bar and had ended up dumping all of her worries on him. "And she still doesn't have her happy face back. You know, the one she had before TK went away?"

Josh was chewing his thumbnail, thinking. "Do you know what she needs?" he said. "A surprise dinner! You know, with awesome comfort food?"

Anya laughed. "You're just saying that because you're hungry."

"Okay, yeah, usually true," Josh agreed sheepishly. "But I kind of feel like Kit just needs something that says *home*. Hey! What if we threw her, like, a real Thanksgiving dinner? You know, we'll invite us and Nav and Will?"

Nav joined the group just as Anya said, "I like it!"

"Yeah, and then, *bam!* We kill it," Josh said, "by making her turducken!"

Anya had never heard of turducken. A glance at Nav told her that he had no idea what Josh was talking about, either. "Okay, now you're speaking another language."

Josh's explanation came with comically accurate hand motions. "It's a chicken. In a duck. Stuffed inside a turkey. It's good!"

"That sounds . . . ambitious," Anya said. "We don't have the whole day—"

Nav cut in. "Who says that you don't? I could call us a car, take her into the village to keep her busy—"

"But you'd need a permission slip and then a guardian—"

Nav stopped Anya again. "Leave that to me. If anyone asks, say that you *just* saw us." He winked and left.

"Pie!" Josh shouted, apparently still wrapped up in his food daydream. "We could have pie!"

"Small reality check. How are we going to cook all this?"

Josh waved his arms around. "That is a problem for my future self, okay? Don't rain your logic down on the artist! Wait—oh, oh! Mashed potatoes! Oh, and gravy, we could have gravy!"

If either of them had known that Elaine was listening in, they might have lowered their voices. As it was, Elaine heard all about their plans, especially about who they were going to invite.

Her name had not been mentioned.

Kit was so excited! *I'm going to see TK!* she thought as she pawed through a pile of clean laundry. She'd been so busy yesterday that she didn't have time to fold it, and now she needed to find her warm sweater and her cap for her "adventure" with Nav. And her jacket, she definitely needed that. Where was it, anyway? "Have you seen my jacket?" she asked Anya.

Anya was busy preparing for her day, too. "It's over there on your vanity," she answered, her head in her wardrobe.

"What are you doing today?" Kit asked her.

"Nothing," Anya said quickly as she backed out of the wardrobe. "Why? What have you heard?"

"Nothing," said Kit. "Why are you being weird?"

"I'm not." Anya closed her wardrobe. "Why are *you* being weird?"

Something was definitely up, and Kit was curious. She had learned long ago that the best way to learn a secret was to offer one first, so she said, "I'm kind of doing something with Nav, but I don't know if I'm supposed to tell you what."

"Ah, I already know! He's taking you out into town so that we can make—" Anya slapped her hand over her mouth.

"Make me what?" Kit urged.

Anya lowered her hand. "We're making you a turducken. To cheer you up about TK and stuff." Guilt flashed in her eyes. "I promised I'd never lie to you again, and I guess that makes me terrible at keeping secrets. Promise to act surprised?"

Kit laughed. "I will be, if you actually pull that off!"

"It does sound a bit challenging," said Anya, but enthusiasm grew in her voice as she went on. "But Josh assures me that cooking one is 'no problemo'! So Nav's in on the turducken plan. We just really wanted to cheer you up."

Kit smiled so hard her cheeks hurt. Oh, that rascally Nav! One secret plan on a Saturday afternoon wasn't enough for him. No, he had to get involved in *two*, and he actually made them dovetail. All she could say to that was, "I can't wait for dinner!"

Anya furrowed her brow. "But seriously? I think you'll be waiting a long time, because I'm not quite sure I trust Josh on the whole 'no problemo' thing."

"Probably smart," said Kit. "You're so good!" She gave Anya a hug.

Sally Warrington loved teaching at Covington, but she loved Saturdays even more so.

Every Saturday morning, she spent extra time in the dining hall after most everyone else was gone. She would sit at the head table and enjoy two warm croissants, a nice hot latte, and the weekly newspaper crossword puzzle. She wasn't a crossword fanatic or anything. The village newspaper just happened to print unusually interesting crossword puzzles. And unlike too many of her literature students, she enjoyed challenging her intellect once in a while.

When Rudy bumbled in with a laptop and sat down right next to her, she didn't mind. She was willing to share her Saturday morning ritual with anyone, especially her favorite cowboy.

"Good morning," Rudy said. "I see you're enjoying some peace and quiet. Don't worry—you won't even know I'm here."

Sally gave him a smile and went back to her crossword while Rudy opened up his laptop. *Boop beepbeep bop!* the machine signaled loudly, and a recorded voice blared, "It's time to play Goody Grab!"

Rudy jumped in his seat, then chuckled in embarrassment. "Sorry. Clicked the wrong doohickey."

Sally certainly understood that. How many times had she herself clicked the wrong doohickey? Once that wrong doohickey had caused her to wipe out her entire semester class schedule. After that she'd made a point of learning more about computers and their many, many doohickeys. "Do you need some help?" she asked Rudy.

"Nope, all good," he answered, eyes glued to the laptop screen.

Sally went back to her crossword, only to hear two seconds later, "Are you sure you want to delete all files?"

Rudy made a rather high-pitched noise of alarm and jabbed at the keys.

"Delete all files," the computer confirmed.

"Quite seriously," Sally said, "I don't mind helping."

"Nah, I got it."

Rudy was such a typical guy, rejecting any help when it came to operating a machine. It seemed to Sally that quite a lot of men insisted they could operate any piece of machinery near them, as if they could suck the knowledge out of thin air and then perform the needed operations perfectly. She had witnessed the results of several such situations, and they rarely came to satisfactory conclusions. In fact, they quite often led to entertaining disasters involving parts falling off and lots of smoke. Her friends told her that it was "a guy thing." She considered it a terribly cute guy thing. Nothing amused her more than watching a grown man fighting a hopeless battle with a mechanical object.

She took a bite of croissant followed by a sip of latte and went back to her crossword.

"Oh, I see," the computer blared. "Call 403-555-2846."

Sally sighed. This was the last straw. Rudy needed help, and she was going to help him. "Will you please allow me to . . . ?"

Her voice trailed off. Rudy was on the Video Chat Express page apparently trying to call Sarah_77, an attractive young woman wearing a cowboy hat. Sally might have gasped. She wasn't entirely sure if she did or not.

Rudy slammed the laptop shut.

Sally stared down at her newspaper, not sure what to say. She liked Rudy, a lot, and she had been under the impression that Rudy liked her, too. They'd had dinner together, and they got along so nicely.

So who was Sarah_77?

A very awkward silence passed before Kit barged into the dining hall.

Kit was making a beeline for the buffet table when she heard her dad's voice. "Hey, Kit!" He was sitting at the head table next to Sally, and he had his laptop. "You were going to give me some help with that *thing* . . . ?"

Kit's mind was on TK. Nav was waiting for her outside. She'd just come in to grab snacks before the big adventure started. What was this about a *thing*?

"I need to make a call?" Rudy prompted.

Oh! *That* call. Yeah, Kit had promised to help him call somebody back in Montana because her dad could never make heads or tails out of his computer, but now was so not the time. "I can't, Dad," she said hurriedly. "I have a really urgent study sesh. You know, midterms, am I right?" She started stuffing her bag with muffins and apples and croissants, babbling, "I have to reread Austen and Brontë and Bieber . . ." She aimed that last part at Sally, who adopted her stern teacher face. Kit pointed at her. "Aha! Just making sure you were listening!"

When her bag was bulging with food, she noticed that Rudy and Sally were exchanging raised eyebrows.

"I, uh, I get really hungry when I read Dickens," she said. "'Please, sir, I want some more!' More carbs. It helps me concentrate. Anywho . . . bye!"

Before they could say a word, she rushed out to meet Nav, thinking, *TK, here I come!*

Sally observed Kit as the teenager raced out of the room, wondering if she would ever understand the Bridges family. Rudy was enough of a puzzle. Kit, she decided, was in a category all her own.

Rudy stood up with his laptop. "Enjoy your crossword, Miss Sally," he said. She thought he sounded out of sorts, but then he said, "By the way, five across is *apologetic*."

Sally had been trying to figure that out for some time. She checked the clue—he was right! "Oh!" she said, then pulled her pencil out of her hair bun and scribbled down the letters in the correct boxes.

At least one puzzle was solved.

Chapter 13

GOOD LUCKIN' WITH THE TURDUCKEN!

So far Anya and Josh had managed to collect a few ingredients for their turducken: a small Cornish game hen, a couple of carrots, celery, an onion, and some kind of roundish leafy green vegetable . . . thing . . . that neither of them could identify but, hey, they were sure they could work with it. At this point, the problem wasn't so much obtaining ingredients as finding a place where they could turn those ingredients into Turducken Delight.

"The cook says we can't use the kitchen," Anya informed Josh as they walked down the corridor of the main building. "Liability reasons or whatever."

"Are you kidding me?" Josh asked, toting their bag of foodstuffs. "What does he think we're going to do?"

"Burn down the kitchen."

"Us? As if we're ever going to burn down . . . Actually, yeah, he's got somewhat of a good point there . . ."

"So what do we do? What's the next plan? Do we cancel?"

"No! We just kind of go stealth, you know? Find another place, another stove . . ." Josh trailed off as Rudy and Will approached them. "Ah! Mr. B.!"

Anya couldn't figure why Josh would bring their equestrian instructor into the conversation until she heard his next words.

"Do you think we could use your camping equipment?"

"The what now?" Rudy asked. "What part?"

"Oh, just the part that heats up and cooks food."

"I'm not lending you a stove unless I know—"

"What on earth!" said Lady Covington, exiting her office just in time to hear Josh's request. Elaine was with her.

Anya quickly explained, "We'd like to cook Kit

a Thanksducken . . . turken . . . chickey . . . ?" She looked to Josh for help, but he stayed silent, looking amused by her floundering. "Oh, we just call it a three-bird roast!" Anya finally concluded.

"Why would you be cooking such a thing for Katherine?" Lady Covington asked.

Just then, Elaine spoke up. "I was just asking Lady Covington where Kit was. Have you seen her?"

Uh-oh. Anya gave Josh a *don't answer* look and said, "Our room," just as he said, "The dining hall." Anya wanted to smack him, but she also wanted to keep control of the situation, so she said firmly, "Music classrooms!" just as Josh said, "Library!"

Then Josh quickly muttered, "Uh, the music classrooms."

Anya was sure Lady Covington would scold them for lying, but the headmistress only drew in a long breath. "I see. Well, if you'll excuse us?" She began to guide Elaine away.

Josh asked, "But can we use the cooktop thing?"

"I'll leave that to Mr. Bridges's discretion," the headmistress answered.

Rudy told Josh, "Come by and pick it up later." He and Will resumed their way down the hall, and so did Lady Covington and Elaine—until the head-mistress turned to say, "Oh, what time is dinner?"

Anya paled. "Seven?" she blurted out.

At least Josh didn't argue. "Yeah," he said, sounding a little faint. "Yeah, seven."

"Excellent," Lady Covington said with a smile. "I'll see you then." She glanced at Elaine, then back at Anya. "Oh. Have you forgotten? It's rather rude to discuss a party in front of somebody who's not invited. Unless, of course—"

"Yes!" Anya hastened. "Elaine! I've been looking for you everywhere. We'd like to invite you."

Elaine appeared uncomfortable, but she managed a small smile. "See you at seven."

Josh nodded. "All right!"

"Excellent," Lady Covington concluded, and she and Elaine left.

Once they were gone, Josh turned on Anya. "Anyone else you'd like to invite? First-Formers? People from the village? Your Blurter followers?"

He seemed annoyed, but Anya could only laugh at him. If he insisted on getting them into these kinds of predicaments, at least he could be cheerful about it. They'd just had a near miss with the headmistress!

The last three minutes could have gotten them into loads of trouble, but instead, they were free to use Rudy's camp stove. And that meant that they had official permission to give this crazy dinner party for Kit . . . and Elaine . . . and Lady Covington herself . . . and they still didn't really know what they were doing and . . .

Oh, dear.

Will followed Rudy into the tack room and sat down at the desk. Rudy opened his laptop and Will began to type.

"I sure appreciate you helping me out with this," Rudy told him.

"Oh, it's fine," Will said, continuing to type. "It's a doddle." He tapped the final key. "There!" He'd brought the Video Chat Express program back to its log-in screen so that Rudy could start over. Whatever Rudy had done before this had frozen the app. "Just type in your password."

Rudy bent over and, with a precision-controlled cowboy index finger, slowly tapped out, "R-U-D-Y 1-2-3-4." He said each letter and number out loud as he tapped it. "It's the same one I use for everything."

Will didn't consider himself a computer expert, but he knew that using the same password for everything was not the wisest move. "That's a little bit concerning," he told Rudy, and was ready to explain why when he noticed that the program wasn't opening. "Oh, now you have to press Enter," Will said. He tapped the Enter key, and the program opened.

"Hey, I did it!" Rudy crowed happily. "You know, Kit must have showed me how to do that seven times, but I never got it until now!"

"Maybe you're just an eighth try kind of guy," Will replied. He felt good. It was nice to be able to help Rudy—and when it came to computers, Rudy obviously needed all the help he could get.

Rudy was smiling, still savoring his success. "If you can teach me how to do this, you can do anything," he said.

"What, you think I'm an eighth try kind of guy as well?"

The mood of the conversation seemed to shift as Rudy commented in a softer tone, "Some things in life are worth fighting for, son."

Before Will could reply, the laptop *booped* and a chat window opened to reveal a pretty young woman sitting in what appeared to be a tack room very much like theirs. "Hey, Rudy Bridges!" she said in greeting. "I can't believe it's really you!"

Will gave up the chair so that Rudy could sit down in front of the laptop. "Sarah!" Rudy said. "How are you? It's been too long."

Will wondered what the call was about. This Sarah person sounded like a good friend that Rudy hadn't seen in a long time. An old classmate, maybe? An old girlfriend? The idea made Will chuckle as he left his teacher to his conversation.

Finally! Kit thought as she and Nav set off on their adventure. *I'm finally going to find TK!*

She and Nav walked at a brisk pace down a side road leading out of the Covington school grounds. Nav had arranged for a car to pick them up there. It was brilliant! Lady Covington wouldn't see the car, so she would never know they had left. Actually, Nav had chosen a spot so far down the road that *nobody* was likely to see them. All the better!

"I am so excited!" Kit said, hopping as she walked. "And you are a miracle! You made such a great plan!"

When they reached the car, Nav, smooth and suave as usual, opened the passenger door for her, saying, "A Nav Andrada plan always works."

"Except when it doesn't," Kit would have said if her mouth hadn't suddenly fallen open. *Lady Covington was sitting in the car.*

"Going somewhere?" the headmistress asked them in a cool, crisp voice.

"How did you—?" Kit began.

"Students may leave the premises only with written permission and accompanied by a chaperone. Unless you would like me to accompany you to wherever it is you're going?"

Kit didn't know what to say. How had they gotten caught? Someone must have seen them, but who? When? How? *Oh, what does it matter?* Kit thought angrily. *Plan scrapped.*

"A week's detention," Lady Covington declared. "I trust that during that time, you will see the error of your ways. Now, straight inside."

"Yes, ma'am," Kit replied.

Nav nodded to the headmistress and closed the car door.

As they started back up the road, Kit saw how dispirited Nav felt. She nudged him. "Meet me in the stables in fifteen minutes. It's time to try a Kit Bridges plan."

Nav grinned.

Anya was beginning to think that Josh Luders was totally and utterly barmy.

They'd set up their "kitchen" in a science classroom so that they would have a nice big table to work on. They arranged all their ingredients and cooking utensils on the table, along with Rudy's camp stove, a timer, and a lamp.

It made a dismal sight. Anya tried to keep up her spirits, but how in the world were they going to turn this sad little collection into Turducken Delight? "I think we're up to seven people," she told Josh. "Is Will coming?"

"If there's food and Kit, he's coming," Josh replied as he put on a cook's apron. "Hey, it's going to be okay. I mean, we have lots of"—he gestured at the table—"parsley."

Anya picked up a huge bunch of the herb. It was enough to make into a flower arrangement! "Why *do* we have so much parsley?" she asked.

"It was, like, the only thing left in the school garden, along with"—Josh picked up what looked like a hunk of gnarled wood—"whatever this is."

Anya groaned. He didn't even know what it was! How could he cook with it if he didn't even know what it was?

He must have felt her panic, because he assured her for the twentieth time, "It's going to be fine."

"Really? Because I'm thinking we might have a slight problem unless we're only serving starters to a small child." She picked up one of the carrots. It wobbled sideways, looking long past its prime.

Josh plucked it from her hand. He was getting nervous, she was sure of it, because his voice was tense as he said, "Trust me."

Lonely. What an awful word.

Elaine would never use that word when referring to herself, even though it was true. Today was a beautiful Saturday afternoon, and she couldn't find a single person to take a ride with her. Everyone was busy doing something with someone else, even Peaches, who claimed she'd promised to help her friend Minnie Minister groom her plush animal collection.

"She has so many of them!" Peaches had said. "And her Plucky Panda bites, so two people are required for safety reasons."

Elaine had cut her off there.

She had tacked up Thunder and was now out riding by herself. And yes, it was lonely. For a horse, Thunder made a wonderful companion, but she didn't think of him as a friend, so she was feeling pretty low by the time she took the trail heading back to the school.

This trail ran behind the stables. As she rode Thunder at a lazy walk, she heard familiar voices in the stable's rear courtyard. She gently pulled Thunder to a stop and peeked through the fence to see—who else?—the cowgirl. She was straddling a bicycle and holding another one steady while Nav nervously stared at it.

"Are you sure about this?" she heard Nav ask Kit.

"Yeah, hop on," Kit said. "We've got places to be."

"I'm just, um, I, um . . ."

Elaine's interest grew. She'd never seen Navarro Andrada act so awkward before. What was going on?

"I mean, we shouldn't leave the property so soon after getting caught," Nav finally said.

They'd gotten caught? By whom? And what had they been doing? Elaine gave Thunder a soothing pat, hoping he would stay quiet so she wouldn't be discovered eavesdropping.

"Well, I'm going to find TK. Today. If you don't want to come, just tell me where he is." Kit had her helmet on and was ready to go. She waited impatiently while Nav fumbled with his helmet and almost let his bike fall over. "Come on—clock's ticking."

Nav straddled his bike and gingerly placed one foot on the pedal. He held his body in a weird stance that put him completely off balance. Elaine had begun to suspect what Kit said out loud: "Wait—do you not know how to ride a bike?"

Elaine had heard enough. So the cowgirl thought she was going to find her donkey, eh? She wasn't going anywhere if her guide couldn't ride. Elaine urged Thunder to resume walking as Kit grumbled, "Well, that makes the Kit Bridges escape plan a little bit tricky."

Kit heard the sound of nearby horse hooves. Somebody was riding the trail behind the stables, but she presumed that whoever it was would have no interest in what she and Nav were doing. And what were they doing? "We're going to have an impromptu bicycle riding lesson!"

"Oh, I'm not sure that's a good idea," Nav protested. "Perhaps we should—"

"La la la la la, I'm not listening!" Kit sang. "This is TK we're talking about, remember? I need your help to find him, and that means that you are going to ride that bike. Just think of it as a really skinny horse. With wheels. And pedals."

During the next twenty minutes, Kit did her best to remember what it had felt like as a child when her father had taught her to ride her first bike. "You have to keep a certain speed, though," she instructed Nav as he wobbled along, his expression one of fierce concentration. "If you go too slow, you're going to tumble and fizzle off."

"Got it," said Nav. He managed to ride around

in a circle, but the circle was too small, and he almost toppled. Kit suggested he make the circle bigger, so he tried again.

"How do you not know how to ride a bike?" she asked, following along with him in case he lost his balance again.

"My father would always say that's why we had drivers," Nav explained, struggling to keep the handlebars steady. "He would buy me horses, but he drew the line at a bicycle."

Nav's wobbling got worse. "Don't oversteer," Kit instructed him. "And don't overthink. You'll get it." She kept up with him as he made yet another circle, and this time he didn't wobble as much. "There you go! There you go—that's it!"

And then he fell over.

In the classroom kitchen, Anya and Josh peered into the toaster oven. They had intended to use Rudy's camp stove, but they'd discovered that camp stoves don't come with a roast setting. So they'd hunted around and located a toaster oven, but although it had a roast setting, their Cornish game hen didn't seem to be roasting—or even toasting, for that matter—very well.

"It's raw!" Anya cried, examining the little bird. "It's totally raw!"

Josh rubbed his hands uneasily. "How much time do we have?"

"A few hours! Josh, I just, I—"

"Uh-uh!" Josh stopped her. "Don't be a hater. Okay? Trust in the power of Josh."

Will burst into the room. "Have you guys seen Kit? I've been looking for her everywhere. I've got this idea to make her more comfortable on another horse."

"She was studying," Josh told him.

"On Saturday? Right." Will clearly didn't believe that, so he asked, "Anya?"

Anya refused to fib anymore. She felt as though she'd said nothing but fibs all day. Josh had a tendency to warp reality like that. She clapped her hand over her mouth and shrugged.

"Oh, you, too? Right. Well, if you see her, send her to the stables?" Will peeked into the toaster oven at the small bird. "Josh, are you going to serve one of those for each of us?" Will burst out laughing and left.

Anya frowned after him. "Josh, I think it's time to admit defeat and call the pizza man."

"A Luders never surrenders!"

"Is that, like, your family motto?"

Now Josh laughed. "It should be. We get into a lot of surrender-ish situations."

He got busy doing something important-looking with the onion while Anya picked up the huge wad of parsley and glared at it.

Chapter 14

NIGHTSHADE AND PARSLEY AND HENS, OH MY!

Kit was so excited to be on her way to TK that she even felt cheery about Nav's wonky bicycle riding. In truth, he improved with every mile. He kept up with her well enough, yelling, "Whoa!" or "Oh, no!" whenever the ground got bumpy, but he maintained control and fell off only once, when a loose rock made his wheel slip. Kit was afraid that he'd hurt himself, but Nav seemed to know how to fall safely almost as well as he knew how to ride (a horse, anyway).

"Now look at you!" Kit encouraged him as they rolled along a grassy path. "You're looking great! Almost ready for the Tour de France!"

Nav laughed as they stopped, his bike jerking when he squeezed the brakes too hard. "Might need a few more tips," he admitted.

Kit scanned the terrain. "Are we close?"

"Let me check my sat-nav." When Kit looked at him funny, he said, "You would say PGS."

"GPS," Kit corrected him. She watched him dig through the stuff in his backpack to find the device. When he pulled it out, it was dripping. "I would also say don't give your GPS a bath."

Nav was not pleased. "Must have happened when I dropped my rucksack in the puddle."

Kit reached into her jeans pocket for her cell phone. Her hand felt only fabric. "Oh, man, I must have left my phone in the tack room! How are we ever going to get there?"

"I think we might have a secondary disaster," Nav said, and he lifted a formless wad of dripping ex-croissant from his bag. "A snack-based disaster?"

"Okay, so now what?"

"Well"—and Nav took his helmet off—"I refuse to give up. It's simply not in my nature."

That made Kit smile. "And that is why we're friends, Nav Andrada," she said.

Nav maintained his cool, studying the sun. "The stables are due north," he said, "and that is north." He pointed. "We'll just have to take it as the crow flies."

"Take a lovely walk through the super-dense

woods?" Kit said hesitantly, squinting at the line of trees that lay due north.

"Call it a shortcut."

Kit shrugged and set her bicycle beside a tree. It would be far too difficult to attempt to steer their bikes through thick brambles and heavy leaf litter. They could come back for them later, after they'd found TK.

Will walked briskly out of the main building, still chuckling over Josh and Anya's cooking fiasco and curious about what would end up on Kit's Thanksgiving table at seven o'clock that evening. If that chicken was anything to go by, Kit and the guests would be lucky to end up with a single mouthful of underdone meat and a carrot stick. Oh, and parsley. He'd seen lots and lots of fresh parsley on the make-shift prep station.

He went to Rose Cottage, trotted up the stairs, and knocked on Kit's door. Nothing. He knocked again.

"She's not in there."

Will turned to see Elaine. "Do you know where she's gone?"

"With Nav. I saw them leave the school together a couple of hours ago."

"How do you know?"

"I saw them take off on bikes. Probably gone to London so we all have to panic for a couple of days. I thought I should tell Lady Covington."

"Why?" Will asked. "Why would you do that?"

Elaine answered as if it were obvious. "Because rules are rules." Which apparently meant to her that rules were to be obeyed and that she was allowed to snitch when they weren't.

Will didn't understand that. In his experience, rules had very little meaning, except to make life more difficult than it already was. "Do you really love rules that much?" he asked, hoping for a serious answer. This wasn't the first time Elaine had *ruled* her way into someone else's business.

Elaine seemed to consider the question, and her face softened. She looked down at her shoes. "No one asked me to the dinner. I mean, they did eventually, but only after Lady Covington made them."

Will nodded, grateful for her honesty. He decided to respond with equal honesty. "Well, sometimes you can be a little tough to approach." He tried to make his voice convey sympathy, because he knew that Elaine wasn't a mean person. She was just highly motivated, and sometimes she let it take her in the wrong direction.

On this occasion, she surprised him. "But sometimes the person you don't invite has gone to an accredited cooking school every half term," she said. "And actually likes to help! Sometimes that person can make a beef Wellington and a lobster risotto and a chocolate chestnut roulade that would make you weep."

"I'd really like to try that one day."

Elaine seemed to be on a roll. "It's so good," she said, "that the tears you cry are real chocolate!"

Will laughed. Elaine was so passionate about her feelings on this issue! He rarely saw her like this. He liked her this way. And the chocolate tears comment was funny!

She shifted her stance from one foot to another, suddenly looking vulnerable. "I, um . . . I don't mean to be tough to approach."

It was in that moment that Will felt only affection for Elaine. Yes, she usually drove him nuts, but maybe she had a good heart. And if her skills in a kitchen were really that good, Josh and Anya desperately needed her talents. "Why don't we see if there's anything we can do to help?" he suggested.

Elaine smiled.

Kit waited anxiously near the foot of a hill. Nav had insisted on going up to get a "layout of the land," though Kit would have preferred if she had gone and he'd waited. This woodsy environment wasn't really his thing. Still, he was doing his best to be helpful, and Kit considered him to be quite the gallant gentleman.

He reappeared at the top of the hill and clambered down. His pants were soaking wet.

"What happened?" Kit asked.

"Well, I couldn't see as far as I thought I might. Then I had a small disagreement with a river. But I did find these!" Nav held out a handkerchief full of fresh berries. He was obviously trying to make up for ruining the snacks she'd brought, as well as killing the GPS and getting them lost. Kit found his efforts endearing, but his almost desperate desire to please her also activated her Bridges prankster gene.

"Oh, we can't eat those," Kit said after looking the berries over.

"Not even the red ones?" Nav asked. "I could have sworn I'd had these before."

"Oooooh, no!" Kit said. "Not those, either."

"Forgive me," he said as they resumed walking. "I'm not trying to poison you. I admit I'm a little bit out of my element here."

"There is nothing to forgive," Kit said. "We just grew up doing different stuff. My family used to do survival weekends all the time back home. You have better talents. You found TK!"

The kind words didn't seem to make Nav feel any better. "For now, I've just found a way for us to be stranded and starving in the middle of the woods."

Okay, it's time, Kit thought. *Nav is at his lowest.* She let her Bridges prankster gene take control. Acting like she was starved, she grabbed the handkerchief, took some of the berries, and gobbled them up. "I don't think I've ever actually tried these guys before," she commented, chewing. "Maybe they're fine." Then she bent over, clutching her stomach and making the most disgusting choking sounds she could manage.

Nav's face paled. "Kit!" he yelled as she gagged. "Kit! Why did you —? What do I —?"

Kit straightened back up and grinned at him. "They're all just whortleberries, and they're delicious."

"Not funny!"

"Ah, c'mon." Kit laughed. "It was a *little* funny."

They were interrupted by a horse's whinny. A very familiar horse's whinny.

Kit jerked her head toward the sound. "Is that —?" She gasped and started running.

Nav took off after her.

They ran until they saw a sign: ARMSTRONG STABLES. The land beyond the sign was surrounded by a tall rock wall, but Kit knew — she *knew* — that TK was in there. They'd found him!

They followed the wall for several minutes. It seemed to go on and on and on. "Oh, why does it have to be such a big wall?" Kit whined, desperate to see over it but unable to jump high enough.

"There's no gate," Nav complained.

Kit wanted to pound the wall down with her bare hands. "How do we get in?"

"We could try walking the perimeter of the property," Nav suggested, "but it's immense."

"How could we have come this far and gone

through this much and still not get to see him?" Kit tried jumping up and down again, just to get a peek, but the wall was simply too high. She pressed her hands up against the cold rock barrier. "I'm here, TK. . . ."

Nav found a low spot on the wall. "Kit, let me give you a boost. At least you'll be able to see him." He bent down and laced his fingers together.

The ultimate gentleman! Kit thought gratefully. She put her foot in Nav's makeshift stirrup and peeked over the wall. "I see him!" she cried.

There he stood in the middle of an enormous green field, gazing over his domain, his tail arched and his long mane ruffling in the breeze. *He's so beautiful,* Kit thought, hopeless with the longing to reunite with her friend. "TK!" Kit called, waving.

The second TK heard her voice, his head swung around and his ears swiveled forward. He took a hesitant step, then broke into a full gallop, heading directly for her.

With effort, Kit lunged upward and got most of her body up and over the wall. She dropped down the other side and started running full-tilt toward TK.

Kit Bridges and her wild dancing horse met in the middle of the green field. TK pranced the last few paces and stopped, snorting a happy greeting, while Kit reached out to pet him—

"What do you think you're doing?" someone shouted furiously. "That horse is dangerous!"

Kit had no choice but to run as the angry figure advanced. *I didn't even get a chance to touch him!* she thought, taking one last loving look at TK before sprinting back to the wall.

"Stop!" The stable hand ran after her while pulling out his mobile. "Stop or I'll call the police!" He began punching numbers into his mobile phone as Kit practically threw herself back over the wall.

"I'm not giving up on you, TK!" she cried as she and Nav made their escape.

Anya inspected their little Cornish game hen. It was supposed to be roasted. It had been in the toaster oven for over an hour. Unfortunately, it did not look the least bit cooked. It did, however, appear slightly odd. "Did it shrink?" she asked Josh, mystified. "It looks like it came out of a dryer." The minute she turned back to him, she added, "And you look like someone stabbed you!"

Smears of cranberry sauce covered Josh's apron.

He didn't seem to notice. He just eyed their shriveled Cornish game hen and said, "I have so much respect for my mom right now. Like, she could do this for thirty, no sweat!"

"Can you get her here in an hour?" Anya asked sarcastically. "*Lady C* is coming to this party!"

"I can help." Elaine entered the classroom, followed by Will.

Josh folded his arms and challenged Elaine with his eyes. "Why, dude? We're killin' it here."

"That's not what I heard."

Anya was not in the mood for an ego showdown. She was fully aware that Josh and Elaine didn't like each other. On the other hand, they'd never tried to work together, had they? And for as much as she liked Josh, his turducken plan had swirled down the drain. If they were going to succeed in making a decent dinner for Kit and all the other guests they'd invited, they needed help—even if it came in the shape of Elaine Whiltshire.

"Is that what you're serving?" Elaine asked, barely suppressing a laugh at the sight of their pathetic little hen.

Anya was through protecting Josh's ego. "He said he had turducken in his veins," she said accusingly.

When Elaine giggled, Josh defended himself: "I don't think I actually said that!"

Elaine waved for silence. Anya would have taken it as a typical Whiltshire order, but Elaine grinned as she did it. Behind her, Will was grinning, too. When the orders started coming, they were delivered in a softer tone than usual: "Josh, get me a frying pan. Anya, start dicing. Carrots, onion, whatever you have."

Josh was still in Challenge Mode. "What are we making?"

"Would you ask that of Nigella Lawson?" Elaine demanded.

Anya snickered. She didn't mean to, but she knew who Nigella Lawson was—a famous British journalist, food reviewer, cook, critic, and TV star. Josh had to know who Nigella Lawson was. Everybody in Britain knew who she was!

"Uhhhhhh . . ." said Josh.

Anya sighed. Okay, maybe he didn't.

Elaine pointed to the ingredients as she mentioned them. "We're going to make potato and parsley soup, and a little Cornish game hen fricassee." Giving Josh a reassuring smile, she added, "It's going to be delicious."

Anya wanted that to be true. Oh, if only it would

be true! Could Elaine actually pull it off? "Are you sure?" she asked hesitantly.

Elaine was in Get-to-Work Mode. "Don't just stand there," she barked. "Chop! Dice!"

"What shall I do?" asked Will.

"Wheedle a dessert from somewhere. You need to know which battles to choose." Over her shoulder, Elaine added, "A lesson for you, Joshua."

As Will left in search of dessert, Anya noticed that Josh didn't move. Clearly he did not want to accept orders from Elaine. But then Elaine clapped her hands and cried, "Move!"

"Okay, okay!" Josh said, and jumped into action.

Anya felt hopeful for the first time in hours.

The walk back through the woods was a pain for both Nav and Kit, but the bicycle proved too much for Nav. He finally gave up on his two-wheeled horse when they were still a mile from Covington, and they walked the bikes the rest of the way.

Kit didn't really care one way or another. She felt ripped in two. One half of her danced with elation because she'd seen TK, while the other half of her struggled with anger and despair at having to leave him *again*. "We were so close this whole time!" she complained as they made it back to the school.

"Well, now that you know Lady Covington wasn't being honest, there's something we can do."

"None of this would have happened without you," Kit said. "Thank you so much."

"For what?" Nav replied. "For getting us lost and leaving you more frustrated than ever?"

Kit stopped walking and faced him. "No," she said. "For giving me hope again. Now that I know where TK is, I can start working on a plan to bring him back home." Kit paused. Was that a little red blotch on Nav's cheeks? Was Nav Andrada *blushing*?

"It was really nothing," Nav muttered.

Kit grinned. Yup, Nav was blushing! And she wouldn't let him get away with such modesty. Didn't he understand how amazing he was and how much he had helped her today? "It was one of the nicest things anyone's ever done for me," she told him. She pulled him into a big hug, after which she said, "You're so awesome!" just to see him blush again.

Nav was such a cutie when he blushed.

Will spent an hour asking around the dorms to see if anybody was baking or had sweets on hand. Luckily, Nellie Chatfield's mother had sent her an entire home-baked Irish coffee cake, which Nellie was kind enough to part with in exchange for Will's cleaning her tack for the next week. To Will, it was just one more thing on a long list of tasks he already had to do, so he agreed.

He was on his way back to the makeshift kitchen when he spotted Kit with Nav. They both had bicycles and helmets. Since when did they go on bike rides together? Then, as he watched, Kit gave Nav a hug and beamed happily into his eyes. Will could see Nav's cheeks blush from where he stood!

Will tamped down his emotions and continued on his way.

Chapter 15

ACTING SURPRISED

Anya was shocked. Elaine had transformed the dining hall into a lovely dinner party environment!

First Elaine had determined that their guests would fit at one long table. That meant that all the student tables except one were pushed to the side. Elaine had then instructed Josh and Anya to gather all the candles they could find. They were also to "borrow" all the flower arrangements in the building.

When that was done, Elaine had lit the candles and arranged them throughout the room on tables, shelves, and ledges. The same went for the flower arrangements. After she'd added a couple of well-placed lamps from her own dorm room, the dining hall glowed, sufficiently lit for practicality yet dim enough to create a relaxed dining atmosphere.

But Elaine didn't stop there. She also persuaded the cook to lend her some school china—some *official school china!*—plus silverware. "How did she do that?" Josh asked Anya in disbelief. "The cook thinks *we're* going to burn the kitchen down, but he gives *her* china!"

"She's Elaine Whiltshire," Anya replied.

"Yeah, okay," Josh agreed.

Elaine told Anya to run to Rose Cottage and fetch some black linen napkins from a cabinet that Anya hadn't even noticed before. Where did Elaine learn about this stuff? Had she gone through every room with a magnifying glass on her first day at Covington?

Elaine's final artistic touch was to fold the napkins into swans.

"She is amazing," Josh commented to Anya as Elaine fussed with the table settings. "Like, truly."

Elaine heard him. "Well, don't just stand there like bumps on a log. There's plenty to do. Come on, children!"

"Until she talks," Josh added. "Funny how that works."

Anya nudged him. "It doesn't matter. Did you see what she did with that sad hen? It's, like, gourmet!"

Will came in holding a dessert box. "Here's your cake, just as requested," he said to Elaine.

"Yo, next time, I'll do the whole pastry chef part," Josh offered. "I'm good at that."

Anya smirked at him. "Yeah, I think I'll ask you to prove that in advance of inviting Lady Covington, yeah?"

When Kit made it back to her room, tired, filthy, and yet hopeful, she found a note on her pillow. ACT SURPRISED, it read in Anya's flashy printing. She laughed, wondering what exactly was in store. Could it match her excitement at finding TK?

An hour later, Kit and Nav, both dressed for dinner, arrived at the dining hall. "Yeah, so then her note said to act surprised—" Kit stopped talking. Both of them stopped walking.

The dining hall looked beautiful! And at one central table sat Will, Josh, Anya, Elaine, and Lady

Covington, all of them talking and laughing like one big family.

"And here I am," Kit said, "not having to act...."

"Is she smiling?" asked Nav.

Kit knew he must be referring to Lady Covington, and, yes, indeed, she was smiling! "Is this a trap?" Kit wondered aloud.

She was about to go in when Nav reminded her, "Not a word about TK, not until we can make a plan."

Kit nodded just as Anya spotted them and called, "Kit!"

Everyone at the table turned to watch Kit and Nav enter. "Who did this?" Kit asked, amazed.

"If I'm being honest?" Josh said. "Mostly Elaine."

Elaine smiled modestly. "Everyone played their part. And it's getting cold, so come! Sit!"

Kit led Nav to their chairs as Lady Covington said, "What a surprise. Elaine, this looks, quite simply, delicious."

Kit sat down, beaming. *These are my friends*, she thought in awe. *My friends! And look what they've done, just for me! Nav found TK, and Elaine, of all people, organized everybody to make Thanksgiving dinner!* Kit realized something wonderful at that moment.

She felt at home.

The feeling wasn't solid yet, and big problems still loomed in her life, but right now she had friends, food, and laughter. Life was looking up!

As dinner began, Kit didn't know that her dad was peeking into the dining hall. He watched his daughter smiling and laughing and sharing with her friends, including the Dragon Lady herself. It was a wonderful sight indeed.

"Kit seems very happy," said Sally in a soft voice.

Rudy had sensed her approach. Now she stood beside him looking so cute with a pencil stuck in her bun and her arms full of books. The ultimate English teacher.

"You're doing something right," she added.

"I hope so," Rudy said. "It's been a bit of a roller coaster."

"I'm not an expert, but I *was* a teenage girl, and I think you're getting off rather lightly, actually."

Rudy gave her a grin. "Your kid gets older, and it's harder to make decisions about what might be right for her or you . . ." He shrugged, feeling the weight of his role as father—and not only that but as single parent—very much on his shoulders. He knew Sally was waiting for him to explain himself, but he didn't have the words to do so. He rarely did. "Ah, just ignore me," he said. "Nothing quite so sentimental as an old cowboy."

After dessert was eaten and the formal conversation wound down, Lady Covington thanked her students for a lovely time and made her exit.

Kit and company weren't ready to end the night yet, so they gathered closer over second helpings of cake and talked about the upcoming league gala.

Josh set the tone of the conversation by stating, "Honestly, guys? I feel that we have a shot at making the league gala our own."

"And, Elaine, you've run a clear course for the last six times," Nav put in.

"It's Thunder," Elaine said. "He's been impeccable."

She still had her modesty running at full blast. Kit figured it was because she didn't want to rock the boat, and for that, Kit felt a smidge of affection for Miss Perfect. Only a smidge, though. After all the trauma she'd been through with Elaine, a solid friendship was going to take time. *Then again, all friendships take time, don't they?* she thought. Then, aloud, she brought up a question that had been bugging her. "So what do I have to do to participate in the gala?"

Total crickets, and then everybody responded at once: "What?" and "Really?" and "You're serious?"

"What?" Kit asked defensively.

"I just thought, with TK gone, you might not want to," Anya said.

Kit could deal with that. She had been making such a huge fuss about TK, complaining and whining to everyone who would listen. But now that she finally knew where TK was, her confidence had shot up into the stratosphere. "I know," she said. "But maybe it's time that I just go for it."

Everyone's response differed. Anya looked gobsmacked, Elaine seemed a bit wary, and Josh looked ready to leap into Cheerleader Mode. Kit noticed how Nav grinned, though—he knew she was up to something, and she could tell he was quite curious.

Will was the one who brought up the biggest

practical consideration. "The deadline is tomorrow. You know that, right?"

"Oh, yeah," Kit said. "Of course! . . . Um, the deadline for what?"

"You're not even in the league," Will pointed out. "To compete, you'll have to do an official timed run."

"You'll have to complete the entire jumper course," Elaine chimed in.

Kit turned to her. For once, Elaine wasn't speaking with sarcasm but with what seemed like genuine concern. Kit would have been wowed by that, but the idea of doing the jumper course . . .

And then Nav just had to repeat the worst part by reminding her of the deadline. "Tomorrow," he said.

Chapter 16

AKA THE BIG ONE

R iding class was about to begin. All the students were assembled in the tack room, chatting, while Kit waited at the door. She was hoping to catch a moment with her dad before he started teaching.

She heard him coming and pounced the second he entered. "Can I talk to you, Dad?"

"One sec," he said. He faced the class. "Gather round, gang. The latest standings for the all-schools league are in." He began passing out papers. "As you know, your scores to this point will determine your rankings, which will decide where you compete in the league gala race."

"Yeah, aka the Big One," said Josh.

Rudy nodded. "Exactly. Okay, it should be no surprise that Will, Nav, and Elaine are all in the top five in their division." Everyone burst into applause as Rudy said, "Congrats, you guys."

Kit noticed that Elaine wasn't eating up the praise. Instead she was frowning at her paper. "Individual glory is one thing," she said, "but how is Covington doing as a school? Ah, Luders is in eighth, and Patel is in . . . *twentieth*?" She flapped the paper angrily. "This is a disaster!"

Kit was sure that Josh and Anya did not appreciate the mention of their personal scores. Kit wanted to avoid the same thing, seeing as her name had a zero next to it. "Hey, Dad—"

"As a team, we are in fourth, which is up from the beginning of the term," Rudy said to Elaine. Kit was annoyed at being interrupted, but she understood that the sooner her dad calmed Elaine down, the better everyone would feel, so she kept quiet. "This is a *win*," Rudy went on. "And you two," he then said to Anya and Josh, "still have time to turn this around. Nothing's impossible, not for this team. You've got to remember that. Even with Kit's zero, we've still got a real shot."

"Could we please not call it Kit's big fat zero?" Kit asked. "It's technically a *did not participate*."

Instead of saying something nice to his daughter, Rudy looked past her. "Nav, are you all right? You should be happy about this."

Kit turned to see what Nav was doing. He had his handkerchief in his hand. Then Kit noticed that one corner bore a monogram, SVA. *It's not Nav's,* she thought. *So what's he doing with somebody else's hand-kerchief, and why does he look so upset about it?*

"Yeah," Nav said absently, looking lost in thought. Then he seemed to snap back to reality. "I mean, thank you, sir. Please, could you excuse me?" Clutching the handkerchief as if he wanted to squeeze it to death, he left the tack room.

That seemed to signal a class break. Rudy stepped over to his desk, and Kit grabbed her chance. She hustled to his side and announced, "I brought you a coffee!"

Rudy jumped. "Oh! I didn't see you there."

"Very funny. I wanted to talk to you about something. I want to compete in the gala."

Rudy had lifted the coffee halfway to his mouth. That's where it stayed as he regarded his daughter with wide eyes. "You do?"

"Yes. And I know I have to do an official run because I don't actually have a rank and I know that the deadline is"—Kit made a little helpless gesture—"today."

"Well, it seems as if you've already thought this through."

In all honesty, Kit hadn't thought it through, not completely. She had never ridden in a gala before, and she wasn't sure how she was going to deal with it. All she knew for sure was that she needed to do it. She felt it in her bones. Kit Bridges had to be part of the gala. "So?" she asked.

Rudy thought about it. "Well, we've got a judge down here doing some makeups. I'll request permission to have you included." He smiled and finally took that sip of coffee as if all of this was no big deal.

He's just trying to keep me calm, Kit thought, hopping on her toes in excitement. "Oh, my gosh! Okay, things just got real!" She took a deep breath, afraid that her heart would beat so hard it would burst. "I'm doing this. I'm really doing this, *today*!"

Nav had found the sva handkerchief on the ground in the stable. At first he'd wondered if it could have gotten mixed in with his things, and then maybe he dropped it. But no, there was only explanation for its presence, and Nav didn't like it. It took him a while, but he eventually found the handkerchief's owner near the main driveway, playing a game with Will and Winston. "What are you doing?" he asked as he drew close to the group.

"Playing keepie-uppies," answered Will.

"It's called *ti jian*," Nav corrected him. Most people thought of hacky sack as having been invented in the United States in the 1970s, but he knew it had its roots in traditional Asian games.

Will didn't seem to care. "Doesn't matter what you call it," he said as he kicked the foot bag over to Winston. "Have you seen this guy? He's amazing." Will was referring to the third member of their trio.

Nav faced that member. "To what do I owe this surprise visit, Santiago?" he asked, adding, "And may I see your visitor's pass?"

While Will and Winston continued kicking the foot bag back and forth, Santiago produced his pass. "There you go," he said in a thick Spanish accent. "Our half-term break is a couple of weeks earlier than yours, and I thought of the idea of a quick jaunt to Rome or Buenos Aires, but then I thought, why not visit my favorite cousin, eh?"

Irritated, Nav kicked the foot bag as it flew toward

Santiago. Since he hadn't been aiming, the foot bag sailed high over their heads and landed some distance away.

"Right, mate," said Will. "Well done for ruining a friendly game."

"There are no friendly games, William," Nav replied while frowning at his cousin.

Santiago laughed.

After looking for Nav for some time, Kit found him in the stables. "Okay, the plan is in motion. All I have to do is ride the trial today, which should be super-mad-crazy-easy!" She wrung her hands nervously.

Nav, still holding the mysterious handkerchief, responded with a vague, "The trial . . . ?"

"Because if I earn the right to compete in the league gala, then Lady C might consider bringing TK back! At least, that's my hope." Kit couldn't stand the mystery anymore and asked, "What is that?"

As if snapping awake from a dream, Nav shook his head. "Oh! Uh, nothing. Sorry. You were saying?"

Kit risked coming right out with her request. "Can I borrow Prince? And you, too! I need you guys to get me through the trial. Prince is the only other horse I can even think about getting on."

Nav's eyes suddenly flared with anger. "Are you mad? Not Prince, and definitely not today!"

Kit stepped back. "Whoa. Do you mind helping me pick my head up off the floor? I didn't expect it to be snapped right off."

Nav looked mad, and he seemed to be on a roll. "Look, take my phone, take my saddle—take my private jet anywhere you want! Anything but Prince! I can't part with him, not today!"

Kit was getting concerned now. She had never seen Nav so angry, let alone at her. "Are you okay? You're all jumpy." She wanted to add, "Can I help?" but didn't know what effect it would have. Nav wasn't acting like himself.

He closed his eyes for a moment. When he opened them again, he was close to being normal Nav again. "It's my cousin," he confessed. "Santiago. He showed up this morning, dropping little clues for me to find." He held up the handkerchief. "Last time we met, it ended badly."

Now Kit understood. If there was one thing in life that could make a sweet, composed guy like Nav come totally unhinged, it was family. Parents, brothers, sisters, cousins, aunts, uncles—all of them were precious gifts that made life worthwhile. And they had the power to completely mess up your head just as well. "How badly?" she asked him.

With a glance up at the heavens, Nav declared, "He beat me at cricket."

If Nav weren't so bent out of shape, Kit would have laughed. That was it? A game of cricket? "Ohhhhh," she teased. "So it was super serious."

Nav didn't look like he appreciated her joke. "You don't understand. My father and his father have competed for their entire lives. And now every move, every grade, every match between us is scrutinized! Judged by our families!" Nav clenched his jaw. "It's a rivalry that we were born to play."

"That sounds intense."

Nav said bitterly, "I need to win, to stay ahead. At all times. My father's name depends on it."

Kit didn't know what to say anymore. She couldn't imagine being born into such a position. When Nav left without saying good-bye—something he would never ordinarily do—Kit stayed where she was, wondering how parents could force such a burden on their kids. Poor Nav certainly didn't deserve it.

By now Anya was familiar with Josh's work schedule, so she went to the tuckshop to see him. Ever since their riding class, she had been feeling out of sorts, and she knew that Josh probably wasn't feeling so hot, either.

"That hurt my heart, man," Josh said, referring to that morning's riding class. "I mean, I don't really like being the weakest link. My jumper scores were so killer last time! It's just, my earlier scores weren't as great."

"I know," Anya agreed. "I'm starting to wonder if they only let me win at home because I'm the princess."

Josh vehemently shook his head. "No," he said. "I've seen you jump. You're like—you're like an eagle!"

Anya smiled. "Thank you. And you are a space shuttle! But how do we get to the next level?" That was the big question, and Anya had no clue how to find the answer. She hoped Josh might have an idea.

He considered the question. "I think maybe Elaine's not totally nuts—in some departments," he said. "I've seen her triple-indexed color-coded homework. She's intense! But, dude, she totally runs circles around us. Maybe there's something she knows that we don't." At that, he reached into his bag and slid out several laminated papers. He presented them to Anya.

She took one look and gasped. "This is Elaine's personal training schedule!"

Josh beamed with pride. "Yup. Sneaked it out, copied, laminated, and returned it. Whiltshire's none the wiser."

Anya told herself to never get on Josh's bad side. He had a few talents that she wouldn't want him to use against her, that was for sure. This stunt was impressive. "If only you could use your powers for good," she said, poking him in the arm.

"I did! This is *the one*. This is what keeps her in first place! Sure, she's all about the team and everything, but this is her own gold medal plan."

Anya poked him again. "So what are we waiting for?"

Josh turned the first page to reveal a schedule that would make an Olympic athlete's head spin. The page, entitled "Week 22," broke each of its seven days into a separate category. Each daily task was fully described, timed, and, of course, color-coded for ease of reading.

Elaine also had a Tip of the Week, this week's being "Practice tactical breathing techniques" followed by some kind of coding system that, Anya supposed, told Elaine how, when, and where to practice said tactical breathing techniques. The word FOCUS screamed out in capital letters.

"Whoa!" said Josh, reading. "Yoga? We have to do yoga? Have you ever done yoga?"

Anya heard him but was too appalled at another note. "We have to drink *raw eggs*?"

Josh made a face, then shrugged. "Well, if we want to win . . ."

Anya finished the thought. "We have to *be* Elaine."

They shook hands on it, though Anya stifled a gag at the thought of the raw eggs.

Kit wandered around the practice field, studying the jumper course that had been laid out. This was the course she was expected to ride that afternoon in order to get a league rank. It was a beginner-level course, with most of the jumps low and a couple of them just poles lying on the ground. Kit had to keep reminding herself that this trial ride wasn't so much a competition against other riders as it was a competition against herself. She just had to get ranked. The only person in the way of that was her.

She spotted Will leaning against the fence and went to say hi. He said it first. "Hello. I'm looking for a girl who's looking for a horse?" He held Wayne's reins while the gelding stood patiently behind him, fully tacked up.

"Really?" Kit asked. "Yours?" She didn't want to sound so doubtful, but after Nav's outburst about her borrowing Prince, she hadn't dared to ask anyone else. How did Will know she needed a horse, anyway? *Because who would ride Coco Pie in a league trial?* she answered herself. Coco Pie was a sweetie, but the mare wasn't used to jumping. Kit needed an experienced jumper, and Will knew that. "But Wayne's a daredevil," she pointed out. When Will and Wayne rode a jumper course, they left skid marks behind. Wouldn't Wayne be too spirited for her?

"Nah," said Will with a heart-melting smile. "Nah, that's *me*. Wayne's a big baby. He'll do whatever you want."

Fantastic! Her horse problem was solved! That

only made the next problem feel even worse, and the truth slipped out. "I'm so scared."

"Yeah, I know." Will grinned as Wayne lipped at his collar. Will gave the horse a pat. "But I'll be standing right here, and I'll be holding him. It'll be just like a pony ride, all right? Come on."

Kit took a deep breath and approached Wayne's left side. On a count of three, Will helped hoist her into the saddle. She sat perfectly still for several seconds, getting used to Wayne's height. He was a big horse like TK, and the ground looked like it was a mile down.

"Keep breathing," Will suggested. "It's important. Essential, actually."

Kit hadn't even realized that she'd been holding her breath. She let it out with a weak chuckle, feeling nervous as well as excited. *I got on, and I didn't faint!* she thought, mentally giving herself a round of applause.

"Do you want to take a walk around the course?" Will asked.

Kit had been concentrating so hard on making it into the saddle that she'd forgotten that the purpose of mounting a horse was to ride it. "What if Wayne doesn't like me?" she fretted.

"I can already tell he does," replied Will. "See how relaxed he is?"

"So he's not going to suddenly bolt and go tearing for the trees?"

"No, no." Will gave the horse a loving stroke down his long neck. "He knows this course. Plus, with the trotting poles, it'll feel like a warm-up for him. And he's had loads of riders. He's pretty cool like that."

Kit gripped the reins, appreciating Will's quiet reassurances more than he would ever know. As a rider, Will Palmerston was the epitome of cool. It was nice to know that Wayne shared that quality. "Can he memorize the course for me?" she asked, recalling sessions with Elaine that had involved plastic horses and way too much planking.

Will offered a better idea: "My brother had a really good way of memorizing courses. He'd assign a memory to each jump."

"Like how?"

"Well, like, your first jump is number eight. When I was eight, I had to get stitches—not from falling off a horse or anything. My brother conked me on the head with a rake."

Kit nodded. "That explains a lot." She laughed at Will's insulted expression. "I'm kidding, I'm kidding! Keep going."

"Okay, so when I was six, I had chicken pox. And when I was twelve, I built a tree fort. Your jump order is going to be eight, six, twelve, so that's stitches, chicken pox, tree fort."

"Like remembering a funny story."

"Yeah, exactly. Do you want to try it out?"

Truthfully, Kit answered, "No."

"Great! Let's go for it." Will led Wayne at a trot to the first jump, a series of four poles lying on the ground. Kit tried her hardest to remain calm as Wayne trotted over them easy as pie. "Great!" Will cheered. "Well done!"

"Thanks!" said Kit, dizzy with relief.

"I was talking to Wayne."

Kit never dreamed that she would laugh her way through a jumper course, but that's exactly what she did, thanks to Will.

Chapter 17

FACING THE TRIALS

Josh and Anya were discovering that "being Elaine" wasn't easy.

First Josh had looked up yoga on the web. Now he read out instructions for the tree pose from his mobile while Anya tried to do it. "Vuh-rik-shay-SAY-nuh will improve your balance," he read.

"It's vrik-SHAH-suh-nuh," Anya said, correcting him, standing on one foot with her other foot drawn up to her thigh at a right angle and her palms pressed together at chest level.

"Why am I reading these instructions? You already know it!" Josh complained, though his irritation was a complete put-on. He enjoyed watching Anya get into the tree pose. With her gorgeous long black hair and petite figure, it made her look like a statue of a goddess.

She broke the pose and put her hands on her hips. "I only know how to *say* it. I don't know how to *do* it."

That simply made Josh want to help more. The problem was he had no idea how to do that. So, in typical Luders fashion, he faked it. "Hey, well, just, uh, I don't know, kind of—focus on something. You know?"

Anya snorted at him. "Thanks, guru."

Josh noticed a young man he'd never seen before coming toward them. He wasn't wearing a Covington uniform, but he was very well dressed. "Sorry," the stranger said to Anya in a butter-smooth Spanish accent. "May I?" He held out a hand as if to help her with the pose.

"Who are you?" Anya asked.

The young man gave her a formal bow. "I am Santiago Andrada."

Josh rolled his eyes while Anya said, "No more explanation required." She allowed Santiago to hold her steady as she resumed the pose.

Josh didn't appreciate having another Andrada around. One was bad enough. But while Nav's elegant voice and movements annoyed him at most, there was something about Santiago that Josh found . . . oily. And having him step in like this and act like he knew more than Josh did, well, it was downright impolite.

Josh opened his mouth to protest just as Santiago purred to Anya, "Now send the energy up and out, aiming it toward the heavens." He guided Anya's arms so that she wasn't holding them at chest level but up over her head with her elbows out.

"Oh!" said Anya as she held the corrected pose. "That changes everything!"

Josh had seen enough. "Okay, okay," he told Santiago. "*I'm* the guru. I got this, all right?"

Santiago stepped back with a smug smile. "Okay."

That's when Elaine breezed by on her way to the main building. "I hope you two have a plan to up your rank on the field," she sniped. "We're not going to tank because *you*"—she frowned at Josh—"can't jump and *you*"—now at Anya—"are a scatterbrain." She leaned in threateningly. "Do I need to intervene?"

"Absolutely not!" Josh snapped. "We've *so* got this!" He growled to himself as she left, mystified by how she managed to survive her own ultra-über-perfection day after day. She was such a pest! A talented, high-scoring pest. But a pest nonetheless. At least the Santiago fellow was leaving, though he gave Anya a wink as he did. Josh drew Anya's attention back to him by saying, "Elaine is terrifying. I mean, she's, like, eighty percent of the way to being a full Lady Covington."

"I know," agreed Anya, watching as Elaine disappeared up the stairs. "I'd so rather train with you."

Those words were music to Josh's ears! He dived back into Guru Mode. "Well, then, um, you know, you get . . ." He put his arms over his head and stuck one leg out. "You get up to, uh, to the heavens and, uh . . ." He watched Anya struggle a little, then find her balance and hold the tree pose. "Yeah, like that. Right!"

Josh liked being Anya's guru. Definitely.

Nav had no wish to spend any quality time with his cousin. Still, he couldn't very well ignore him, either. Santiago was the kind of guy you had to keep an eye on. So when Santiago showed up later that morning to "chat," Nav humored him.

They strolled through the stables. "Cousin,"

Santiago said, "do you still have that young buck, Prince?"

"Prince is proving to be an excellent horse," replied Nav, hoping this wasn't going to turn into a my-horse-is-better-than-your-horse competition.

Santiago looked around while walking as though judging the quality of the stable facilities. "Well, wait till you see my new steed. You'll see him in the league gala. He's called King."

The hairs on the back of Nav's neck rose like a dog's hackles, but before he could say anything, Elaine crossed right in front of them with Thunder. "Nicely now, Thunder," she said to the horse as she led him to his stall.

Santiago perked up as she went by. "Who is that?"

"She's not your type," said Nav.

"Bold? Focused? Clearly a winner? I think she's exactly my type."

"She's not interested in boys. She's interested in winning."

"Perhaps she just hasn't met the right cousin yet."

Nav gave up. If Santiago insisted on going after Elaine, of all girls, he was about to get his heart handed back to him in a plastic bag. At least, Nav hoped so.

Oozing aristocratic charm, Santiago sidled up to his prey. "Your hair is like silk," he murmured as if in awe, "and the way that it glistens in the sun? Forgive me, but you took my breath away."

Nav was glad he hadn't eaten recently. Talk about sickening opening lines!

Elaine, however, appeared to be swept away when Santiago took her hand, kissed it, and introduced himself. "Santiago Andrada."

"Um, uh . . ." Elaine stammered. "Th-thank you!"

Nav couldn't stand it. Shouldering his way in front of Santiago, he said smoothly, "Elaine, have I told you how much I liked your design for the league gala? It is the best I have ever seen." Not to be outsuaved, he kissed Elaine's hand, too.

Santiago stepped in front of Nav. "Fancy a hack later?" he asked Elaine. "I hear that you're quite a talent."

Nav, eyes smoldering, locked eyes with Elaine. "She has no time for a casual wander on the trail!" he scolded his cousin. He couldn't believe he was actually wooing Elaine, but he refused to let Santiago win any competition, even this one. "She's the best rider at this school, so she is always practicing," he went on, pitching his voice low and alluring. "And congratulations, Elaine. Obviously Kit is only able to do her trial today because of your work. Shall we go to watch? Together?" He reached for her hand.

Santiago edged around him so that he cut off Nav's reach. "Cousin, please. I haven't the pleasure of seeing Elaine every day." To Elaine, he asked, "May I take you to watch the trial?"

Elaine's cheeks flushed a gentle pink. "Well," she said, "far be it from me to come between family members." She took Santiago's arm on her left and Nav's arm on her right and walked with both of them to the trials.

Anya was helping Kit get ready for her trial. "You've been at it all day," she said reassuringly. "You'll do aces!"

Kit shivered. "I'm just really nervous, especially after my first epic fail."

"You just have to finish the course, and it doesn't have to look pretty. As long as you jump all the jumps, you'll get a rank!"

There was a knock on the door, and Elaine

entered, wringing her hands. "I need your help," she said in a strangely giddy voice. At the word *help*, Kit presumed that Elaine was talking to Anya, not her. She was right. "I need something to wear for Kit's timed trial," Elaine finished to Anya. "Please?"

"Aw, you don't have to get all dressed up for me," Kit teased.

"Actually, um . . ." Elaine shifted from one foot to the other. "I have a date."

Amazed by this news, Kit demanded, "With who?" just as Anya asked the exact same thing. They sounded like twins.

Elaine didn't look like she appreciated the question. "Well, thanks for being completely and utterly gobsmacked by the mere possibility," she snapped.

"Sorry," Kit said.

Anya indicated her wardrobe. "You can borrow anything you like." She paused. "So who is it?"

Elaine gave in. "Well, there are actually *two* boys who might be interested."

What did she do, put love potion in their morning orange juice? Kit wondered. Seriously, though, she was glad. Maybe if Elaine got a boyfriend, she would have better things to do than harp on everyone.

Out on the practice field, the league trials were about to begin. Students gathered at the fences to watch.

Elaine spotted Santiago. It was impossible *not* to notice him with his pristine powder-blue blazer, spotless trousers, and flawlessly coiffed hair. Everyone else wore riding gear, uniforms, or work clothes.

Elaine stopped by Anya first, to thank her again for the scarf she had borrowed and was now wearing. "Kit's getting a rank," Anya said excitedly, "and you're getting a date!"

Elaine would have replied, but her mobile beeped. She pulled it out and saw that Santiago had sent her a text. "Oh, my gosh," she said, reading. "Santiago's had a *botanical garden in Bangkok* named after *me*!"

"No way!" Anya squealed.

Elaine knew that Santiago could hear them. He stood not ten feet away, tapping at his mobile and smiling as he eavesdropped. Elaine also knew that Nav was approaching from behind with a bouquet of flowers, the silly boy. She heard him mutter, "Well played, cousin," as he overheard about the botanical garden. He slumped in defeat. Elaine had the strangest urge to pat him on the head and say, "Nice try, Navarro, but the fastest Andrada wins the race!"

Instead she ignored him and joined Santiago. "Hi," she said breathlessly, giving a coy shoulder wiggle to make sure he noticed her scarf. "I've seen your stats. I'm very impressed."

"It's all about the training program," Santiago said, favoring her with his radiant smile. "I've tailored my own to suit."

"Oh, really? I'd love to hear all about it. I mean, I know you took home first during your school's House Cup. Can anyone even keep up with you?"

Santiago's ego seemed to eat up the praise. "Well, no, not really. Although we do have some strong riders. Paul Rutherford. He tries to keep up, but he has some problems with his release timing."

"Oh? Tell me all about it. It sounds fascinating, truly."

Kit paid no attention to Elaine, Santiago, or anyone else gathered to watch the trials. She walked steadily into the ring, followed by Rudy leading Wayne. *This is it*, Kit thought. *I have this last chance to prove myself. I have to ace this!*

"All right," Rudy said, fishing around in his jacket pocket.

Kit saw the motion. "No! No Ugly Brooch! Not today. I don't think it had its intended effect last time."

Rudy kept fishing in his pocket until he pulled out a necklace. "I got you this instead," he said, placing it in her hand. "For good luck and new beginnings."

Kit sniffled. *No, don't go there!* she thought, admiring the lovely silver horseshoe charm on its shiny silver chain. "Dad," she whimpered, overcome with emotion. "You're going to make me cry! And if I cry, then I can't see the jumps, and even I know that's kind of an important part." She sniffled again while putting the necklace on. The chain length was perfect, allowing the little horseshoe to lie right at the base of her throat. *My dad is the best dad in the whole world*, she thought, touching the charm. *If this doesn't bring me luck, nothing will!*

Rudy, uncomfortable with anything resembling mushy emotions, turned back to practical matters. "Do you feel safe up here?" He patted Wayne's neck. "Wayne's a good horse, but you need to feel safe."

"I hear he's a big baby," Kit replied. "I feel good, Dad." She moved to Wayne's left side, and Rudy gave her a boost into the saddle. She slipped her toes into the stirrups and sat for a moment. Yes, it did feel good. Not great, but good. A few butterflies continued to flutter in her stomach, and her heart pounded, but that was fine. *I can handle it. I think.*

"Now remember what your mom would say," Rudy told her. "Believe you can, and you're halfway there."

"It's going to be great," Kit assured him.

"You know it."

The judge announced, "Next up, rider Kit Bridges."

"This is it, Wayne," Kit murmured. "Let's do it!"

A whinny! Kit suddenly heard the echo of a whinny blow past her ear.

There it came again!

And again, much louder!

Kit's heart pounded for a different reason now. She dismounted Wayne and, dropping his reins, ran as fast as she could out of the ring.

Chapter 18

DREAMS COME TRUE

K it!" shouted Rudy. "What's going on? Kit!"
Kit kept running. Whatever his daughter was
doing, she wasn't going to stop.

Rudy ran over to the judge. "The clock hadn't
started, so there's no time fault, right?" he asked, barging on before the poor man could answer. "Will you
please just move her down in my order and let her go
near the end? I mean, as long as she rides before you
go, all right?"

The judge frowned but nodded, marking his list.
Rudy didn't care if the man felt inconvenienced, as
long as Kit still got her chance. Right now, he had to
find out what had made her bolt like a deer across the
school grounds.

He ran after her.

On the opposite side of the ring, Anya witnessed Kit's sudden mad dash across the field. Where was she going?

Next to her, Josh was busy doing squats.

"Give it a rest," Anya told him. "We're not training right now. We need to go and see if Kit's okay."

"Will went after her," Josh said, putting his hand on her arm. "Maybe you should just, I don't know, give your friend and the cute boy a minute, eh?" He winked and resumed his squats.

Anya tried to see Kit in the distance, but she had disappeared beyond a hill. Figuring she could never catch her now anyway, Anya started doing squats with Josh.

Kit ran. Oh, she knew exactly what she running to, though she couldn't understand how or why it was happening. It had to be a miracle!

And then she saw him.

TK was still far off, galloping toward her with his tail streaming. When he came upon a large pile of thick tree branches in his path, he didn't hesitate but simply sailed over them as if he had wings. Kit could hardly believe it!

TK slowed to a trot, then to a walk. He stopped in front of Kit and lowered his head, whuffling a greeting.

Kit felt numb with shock while at the same time, this whole moment felt to her like cosmic destiny. How could she have ever doubted TK? He had come home to her! He wanted to be with her just as much as she wanted to be with him! "I knew you could find me, boy," she said, petting his forehead. "Ohh, I missed you! And you ran so far—for me! Welcome home!" She pressed her face into his muzzle and gave him a snuggle.

"I have to say, I'm relieved!" Will panted.

Kit turned to see him not far behind her. And bringing up the rear was her dad.

"I thought you'd gone mad," Will continued. "Or bailed or something."

"Oh, no!" Kit said, realizing. "That's what everyone must think!" Her excitement about TK overruled all logic, though, and she blurted out, "But did you see that? Did you see him make it over that jump? It's a sign!"

TK whinnied, nodding his head as if to agree.

Kit pressed her forehead against his. "They cannot keep us apart, bud," she said to him. "We are a team!"

Back at the ring, Elaine showed no interest in Kit's freaky disappearance. She had more important things to do, especially since Nav had come over to vie for her attention with Santiago.

"Would you like a grape?" he inquired, offering one from a bag he was holding.

Santiago pulled a kerchief from his pocket and opened it to reveal star-shaped slices of juicy bright yellow. "Some star fruit?" he suggested.

"Bitto Storico?" Nav insisted, pushing his other hand past Santiago's. A wedge of golden cheese lay in its palm. "It's rare, aged sixteen years, and practically impossible to obtain."

Something to the left caught Santiago's eye. "What's happening there?"

Elaine turned to see Will and Kit leading—was that the donkey? Where had he come from? No matter, Elaine recognized him and just as quickly dismissed him. Boy, girl, and donkey disappeared into the stables.

Nav tucked the Bitto Storico back into his pocket. "If you'll excuse me," he said, and he took off for the stable.

"Please, take your time!" Santiago called after him. "Now, you." He gazed at Elaine. "Tell me about yourself."

"Oh. Well," Elaine said, "I know it's old-fashioned, but I like to have hard copies of all my schedules. So I laminate them and keep them on me at all times. It makes things seem more real that way."

Santiago was charmed by her words. "You really are adorable, you know."

"Oh, I'm not joking," Elaine said. "What, do you take training as a joke?"

"Hardly, no. How else do you think I beat my cousin?" With a tricksy grin, he pulled out his mobile. "I've designed my own app. This is my training schedule. You see, King—he's such an exceptional horse that I only need to do a quick warm-up with him before showtime."

Elaine studied the mobile's screen. Santiago had created an excellent app, though one section confused her. "What's that part there?" she asked, pointing.

"That?" Santiago whispered. "King hates the second jump and often loses time."

"Oh." Elaine put her hand on his arm. "That's such a beautiful app. I mean, I might even consider giving up my laminates for something like that."

Meanwhile in the stables, Kit and Will had TK secure and were quickly gathering his tack.

"Are you sure you want to risk your rank?" Will asked, placing a saddle blanket on TK's back. "Wayne's all ready to go."

"It's a feeling," Kit said passionately. "It's fate! Did you see him make that jump? He can do this!" She stroked TK's neck and said to the horse, "*We* can do this."

Nav ran in. "Whoa! How in the world—?" He gaped at TK as if seeing a ghost.

"I know!" Kit giggled. "I just saw him off in the distance, and I had to go after him!"

Rudy joined them. "Come on, let's go, let's go," he said, taking charge. "We have eight minutes. All hands on deck. Will, get his bridle."

As Will fetched the bridle and Rudy put TK's saddle on, Nav told Kit, "I knew we had to go find him. And now he's found his way back to you!"

"I think we showed him what he had to do," said Kit. "To find us. It wouldn't have happened without you!" She gave him a big hug just as Will returned. She noticed a look pass between Will and Nav, a look that seemed to say, *Let's focus on the task at hand: helping Kit in her hour of need.*

Kit turned back to TK. "This is it, boy. We cannot mess this up. It's our last chance." She caught herself. "I mean, no pressure! But we have to nail this."

Will assured her, "You will."

"I second that," said Nav.

"Thanks, guys. I really don't know what I would do without you."

Like a mother, Will zipped up Kit's show jacket. "Well, you look great."

Nav held out her riding helmet. "And you will *do* great."

Rudy cleared his throat loudly. "You heard me say eight minutes two minutes ago, right? Let's *go*."

When Kit entered the ring astride TK, she heard Elaine mutter, "How does that girl manage to get every single thing she wants?" If Kit hadn't been so nervous, she would have laughed.

For one thing, she didn't agree. True, she had TK again, but the trial still lay ahead. And she had no idea what would happen when Lady Covington discovered TK's presence. No, Kit did not have everything she wanted. She did, however, have a *chance* to have what she wanted, and that was as much as anyone could ask for.

As she guided TK to their starting point, she felt how different it all was this time. TK moved beneath her with relaxed confidence, his head held high, his ears pricked forward. Unlike at the House Cup, he was ready this time, and Kit felt ready as well. That awful fear had left her, and pure excitement bubbled in its place.

"This is it, boy," she whispered. TK swiveled his ears back, listening to her. "Let's *do* this!"

The timer started, and off they went!

TK approached the first jump at a comfortable canter. Thanks to Will's earlier help with Wayne, Kit had already calculated how many strides her mount should take throughout each section of the course. That was part of her score—how accurately she and her mount approached each obstacle and how smoothly they jumped it.

TK and Wayne were about the same size, so Kit's

calculations remained valid. She urged TK to take the first jump at the right point, and he sailed over it without a hitch. Beyond her bubble of concentration, Kit heard a roar of applause from her friends at the rails. Smiling fiercely, she guided TK to the next jump, which TK also cleared effortlessly. More jumps, up and over, up and over.

Now the last two.

TK gathered himself and leaped, tail held high like a banner of triumph. He landed, and Kit heard more loud applause.

One small turn, and the last jump awaited.

TK snorted as he cantered toward it as if to say, "Relax, boss, I got this!" To Kit, everything suddenly shifted into slow motion. She felt TK lift his front legs, and she shifted her torso forward so that she remained balanced in the saddle as he jumped. She felt the power of his hind legs gather and then push up. Girl and horse flew like birds! And then they went down, into a steady landing and the loudest roar of applause yet.

Stunned by success, Kit reined TK back to a walk and guided him to the rails where Rudy and her friends were clapping and cheering. *I'm not dreaming, right?* she thought. *This is real, right? I'm riding TK, and we just blew that jump course away, right?*

Will jogged over and took TK's reins. Kit was grateful—she was afraid she might faint! But not from fear this time—oh no—but from pure wonderful joy! She dismounted as Rudy walked up.

"You made it. You're in the bracket." He spoke calmly, but Kit saw the glint in his eye. She knew exactly what was coming. Father and daughter fell into a touchdown-style victory dance complete with high fives, a few choice dance moves, and a big final "Woo!" Kit basked in her father's delight like it was sunshine. "I am so proud of you," Rudy said. "So, *so* proud!"

Kit couldn't speak yet. All she did was giggle.

Anya leaped into her arms and gave her a tight hug. "That was so thrilling!" Then she put her hand on Kit's shoulder, suddenly looking wobbly. Kit wondered what was wrong, but Anya explained: "Don't let go, okay? I think I might have overdone it with the lunges."

That just made Kit giggle harder.

Anya recovered. "Oh, I'm so proud of you!" she said. "I knew you could do it!"

I knew I could do it, too, Kit thought. *I knew it all along. I just needed the right time with the right horse.*

Kit was summoned to Lady Covington's office before she had a chance to remove TK's tack.

"I'll take care of him," Will offered.

"Me too," said Anya.

"And me!" Nav chimed in.

Kit felt like a queen. "Thank you, all of you. You're the best!" Then she beelined it to the main building and into the headmistress's office. "I don't know how he found me," she told Lady Covington, "or how he even got here, but he did. That has to mean something, right? I could have done the trial with Wayne and it would have been fine, but it was with TK and it was perfect!"

Lady Covington stood with a blank expression. Kit almost panicked. Then the headmistress spoke. "Actually, I'm rather proud of you. Your progress, I mean."

Kit was surprised. "I thought you'd be mad," she said.

"Well, I'm not about to throw a parade for that horse you love—"

"Please!" Kit cut in, about ready to explode from all of the emotions ricocheting around in her. "Please find it in your heart to let him stay?"

"It appears that I don't have a choice," the headmistress confessed. "He escaped from Armstrong Farms, and apparently they were relieved. TK was his usual charming self, and they don't want him back, so for now—"

"Thank you!" Kit cried. "Thank you, Lady Covington!" She almost gave the woman an enthusiastic hug, but she caught herself in time. Bursting with relief and joy and pride and gratitude, she simply gave Lady Covington's arm a cheerful little pat, hoping that didn't cross some kind of line. "You won't regret this!" Kit finished, and she ran out the door.

Lady Covington quietly observed Kit Bridges's rather exuberant exit. The girl was just so wild, so ill-mannered, and even inappropriate at times. She let a tiny smile form on her lips, now that she was alone again. Kit was wild, true, but Lady Covington couldn't help but admire her spirit. And Kit was learning, and the headmistress felt great pride in that.

With a satisfied sigh, she picked up her mobile

and tapped out a number. "Mr. Armstrong?" she said a moment later. "Yes, I just wanted to say thank you and that your check will be in the office this afternoon. Good day."

That night found an extremely happy Elaine in the student lounge. She'd set up her personal laminating machine on a table and was busily laminating a new set of training schedules.

Nav entered and took the seat next to her. "Congratulations," he said. "Our plan was perfectly executed. Santiago didn't suspect a thing." He scanned the materials on the table. "What's this?" He picked up one of the newly laminated papers.

"That is from his app," said Elaine. "He forwarded the whole thing to me. Easier than expected, actually."

"You are a diabolical genius, Whiltshire."

Elaine smiled. "You flatter me, Navarro, but I didn't come up with this plan alone."

Nav matched her smile. "Anything to deal him the massive loss he deserves."

"Oh, he is so full of himself," Elaine agreed. "I

gained us a shocking amount of intel on his entire team. And on his own weaknesses." She indicated the page in Nav's hand.

Riders' Profile Journal it read across the top. Below were all of Elaine's notes on every single rider at Santiago's school. For instance, about Santiago himself, she had written:

NAME: Santiago Andrada

WEAKNESSES: Perfectionist

STRENGTHS: Too many to name—fast and efficient

AREAS NEEDING IMPROVEMENT: Second jump

YEAR STARTED RIDING: 2009

PROBABLE RANK: 1

NOTES: A hair trim before the gala would be nice.

Following Santiago were her notes on the rider who would pose the next biggest threat:

NAME: Paul Rutherford

WEAKNESSES: Eats too much before the show

STRENGTHS: Nice form on trotting

AREAS NEEDING IMPROVEMENT: Speed

YEAR STARTED RIDING: 2009

PROBABLE RANK: 2

NOTES: His jumps are very good.

And on and on it went, a treasure trove of the enemies' stats. Elaine went all giddy just thinking about it!

"They may be one spot ahead now," she told Nav, "but"—she shifted some laminated sheets, tugging one out of the pile—"this is for you."

Nav took it. "You astonish me."

"Whatever it takes to win the league gala, I'm in. But for a second there," and Elaine grinned, "I really thought you were trying to sweep me off my feet."

"Eww, no!"

Her grin vanished.

"I mean," Nav babbled, trying to save himself, "you are, of course, lovely—"

"Please." Elaine had realized long ago that the only thing she could do when so insulted was to simply shake it off. It hurt, but she was used to that. Besides, Nav was correct in that she was not his type, but that only meant that he wasn't her type, either.

"Look, I know he's a big distraction for you at the moment, so I've compiled some pages on focusing. Read it by game day." She handed him a set of laminated pages entitled "16 Easy Steps to Focusing" by Elaine Whiltshire.

Looking curious, Nav took the pages, and Elaine was pleased to see him start to read.

Chapter 19

FROM BEST TO WORST

That night, Kit ran into the tack room. At dinner, she'd been treated to a stream of congratulations from students and staff alike, and she wanted to share it all with her dad. "Oh, my gosh, this is the *greatest*! *Day! Ever!*" she hooted, hopping in front of his desk. "Can you believe it? TK is back, I ace my trials, and — are you ready for it?"

Rudy seemed surprised. "I don't know, am I?"

"Lady C said TK can stay!"

Rudy smiled. "That's great. How about that?"

Caught up in her whirlwind of gleeful success, Kit was surprised by the mildness of his response. "Um, hello? This is huge! Why aren't you more excited?"

"I am," her father replied. "That's great. I couldn't be more proud over how you handled yourself today." Rudy stopped speaking and just looked at his daughter.

"Oh. I know what's coming. The *but*. What's wrong? Why are you acting so weird?" Kit saw the strain in his eyes, even though he quickly looked away, letting out a long breath.

"I just got off the phone with Sarah Payton. We've been talking the last few days. She's the one I had to call from my laptop."

"Sarah Payton from Raindrop Farms?" asked Kit.

Rudy nodded.

"And she's calling to see how we're adjusting to our new fab life? And you told her that it's going great, and we're so glad we made the move?"

Rudy didn't speak.

"Dad?"

"She offered me a job," he said. "Well, not *a* job. *The* job. With an option to buy the whole ranch after three years."

Kit didn't move, not a muscle, not a breath.

"This is what we always dreamed of," Rudy reminded her. "Your mother and I had been talking about this since before you were born. You love Raindrop Farms. This could be—"

"A *disaster*!" Kit cried. "What are you even thinking? We already made the move across the ocean!"

Rudy got up from his chair and began pacing. He seemed at a loss as he finally sat on the edge of his desk. "They always said I'd be the first call they'd make when the time came to sell. And that time is now."

"Now?" Kit echoed. "You want us to leave Covington?" *Now? Now that I have my life again? Now that my best friend has come back, and I've learned to ride again, and I have a home and friends and—and—and everything I ever needed? Except my mom, of course. That goes without saying.*

Kit wasn't sure she'd survive yet another move across the vast Atlantic to start all over again. She wondered if, like a photograph that gets copied again and again, her sharp edges and vivid colors—her very Kit-ness—would start to fade. Just the idea of leaving Covington now made her feel less like herself.

But Raindrop Farms was her dad's dream, and she couldn't deny how much he'd already lost—as much as Kit had found at Covington, at least, and maybe more. So for now, after her father said, "We'll talk about it, okay?" and she agreed, she would bid him good night, hug TK on her way out of the stable, and debrief with Anya when she got back to her room. There were still some unanswered questions—about her mom's background, about how Daisy Rooney's article would portray Covington. And about Raindrop Farms. But for now, she would snuggle into her ah-mazing bed and appreciate each Covington moment as it came. She didn't know how many more there would be.

This book is based on the television series *Ride*.

Copyright © 2018 by Breakthrough Entertainment

First edition 2018

Library of Congress Catalog Card Number pending
ISBN 978-0-7636-9856-0 (hardcover)
ISBN 978-0-7636-9857-7 (paperback)

18 19 20 21 22 23 LSC 10 9 8 7 6 5 4 3 2 1

Printed in Crawfordsville, IN, U.S.A.

This book was typeset in Caslon 450.

Candlewick Entertainment
an imprint of
Candlewick Press
99 Dover Street
Somerville, Massachusetts 02144

visit us at www.candlewick.com